BETRAYAL

By

Denise Hill
Dwuna Henton
Tammy Jackson
Penny Burt

DH Books

BETRAYAL

DH Books published by
DH Publishing Company
P.O. Box 333
Indianapolis, IN 46250

ISBN: 978-1-7336502-7- 4
Book Cover Design: DH Publishing Company
www.DHpublishingco.com

Printed in the United States of America

BETRAYAL

ACKNOWLEGDEMENT

I want to thank God for another opportunity to tell a story through my writing. Also for the opportunity to work with these three ladies on the television series for Betrayal. I hope to have many more opportunities to write with them. As always, I want to thank my support system my son Daniel Powell and my daughter Devin Hill. I hope my readers enjoy part one of the series as much as we enjoyed writing it.
Denise Hill

The words don't express how humble and grateful I am for having the opportunity to work with these amazing women. Bringing our own unique styles together to create something amazing. I thank God first and foremost for the gift and passion to tell stories that inspire and my support system of family and close friends who encourage me to keep going no matter what. Thank you readers for your support! I know this story will keep you on edge of your seat.
Tammy Jackson

I am thankful for my family and friends that kept me encouraged and cheered me on throughout the process and was understanding to my new schedule. Hearing I'm proud of you from my friends, family, and especially my kids, Landon, Ebonyy, and Mahoganyy really meant a lot. Special thanks to Denise for starting a writer's group, and giving us the opportunity to collab on Betrayal. Denise, Penny, and Tammy we've built a sisterhood during our time together and it was so much fun never work.
Dwuna Henton

I would like to thank my co-writers for this awesome experience of collaborating on this project. Thank you for your patience, knowledge, and sisterhood.

To my husband, thank you for your understanding and patience for the time I spent working on this project and away from him.

Last but not least, I thank God for the gift of writing, and for this gift making room for me to express impart and share it with you, the readers.

Penny Burt

BETRAYAL

Prologue

Mr. Taylor, you have a call on line one," Cynthia, Desmond's secretary said.

"Cynthia, hold all my calls for about an hour," He said in between kisses.

"It's your wife."

"I said hold my calls! Desmond yelled.

Cynthia rolled her eyes, "I'm sorry, Mrs. Taylor, but Mr. Taylor is in an meeting. I can have him call you when he gets out, if that's okay.

"Thanks, but don't bother," Stephanie said.

Stephanie sat outside her husband's office as she disconnected the call. She got out of her car and walked toward the office. She did not believe one bit that he was in a meeting. For the last month, she got this same excuse each time she called her husband. Today she would find out what was really going on.

As she made her way inside the building, she waved at Tim at the guard's station. She made her way over to the elevator and rode up to the thirteenth floor.

As she stepped off the elevator and walked down the hallway, she saw her husband's secretary.

"Good morning, Cynthia."

Cynthia smiled, "Good morning, Mrs. Taylor."

Cynthia, a middle-aged Hispanic female who had been with the firm for nine years.

Cynthia watched Mrs. Taylor and didn't stop her as she walked over to Desmond's office door. Stephanie slowly turned the knob, but it was locked. She looked back at Cynthia, who had a key in her hand.

"You didn't get this from me," Cynthia said as she gave the key to Stephanie.

Stephanie winked at Cynthia and moved back over to the door. She put the key in and turned the knob slowly.

"Oh shit! This feels so damn good!" He continued to pump her harder and harder.

Stephanie closed the door behind her. She walked further into the room, and then cleared her throat, "You better get used to that dick because when I am finished with his ass, a dick will be all you're going to get."

BETRAYAL

CHAPTER 1

Candice Spencer, a 35-year-old white female, was considered by many the black sheep of her family. Candice had been in and out of jail since the age of 17, and it always had been behind a man. She has always attracted the wrong men, but when she learned about Desmond Taylor from a friend, she knew he was the right person for the job.

Candice walked inside Starbucks. She scanned the room for the tall, dark, and handsome attorney that stopped there every morning before heading to work.

"Awe, there he is."
Candice walked up to the counter and placed her order, and walked over to his table.

"Do you mind if I sit here?"
Desmond looked up and smiled, "No, go right ahead."

"Thank you. My name is Candice Spencer."
Desmond held his hand out, "Nice to meet you, Candice. I'm Desmond Taylor."

"I see you in here every morning. Do you work nearby?"

"Yes, I do. I work in this building. I work for Kirkland and Ellis."

"Are you an attorney?"

"Yes, I am."

"I bet your job is so interesting. I wanted to be an attorney, but once I dropped out of school, I knew my dream was over."

"It doesn't have to be. You're still young. You could get your GED and go to law school."

"I wish it was that easy."
Desmond decided not to pry.

"Candice." The cashier at the counter yelled.

Candice walked over and grabbed her drink off the counter, and walked back over to the table.

"Maybe we can talk more about what I need to do over lunch or dinner, my treat."

"Let me think about it, and I'll let you know tomorrow," Desmond said.

"Sounds good."

"Well, I have to get to work. I will see you tomorrow."

"You bet."

Candice watched as Desmond walked away, "Damn, he's a looker."

The next day, Desmond and Candice met at the same coffee place.

"How about dinner since I have a lunch meeting today, Desmond said."

"That sounds awesome. Where would you like to meet?"

"It's your treat, so you tell me," Desmond said as he laughed.

Candice and Desmond met for dinner that evening. They talked the entire time. He felt so comfortable with Candice, plus she was easy on the eyes, he thought.

Candice and Desmond met often. One evening, Candice invited him over for dinner. Desmond was a little hesitant to go, but the more he thought about Candice, the more he couldn't wait to be in her company. She had a way of making him feel like he was the best thing since sliced bread.

After dinner, Candice and Desmond moved to the living room and sat on the couch drinking Carlo Rossi Red Sangria wine. Candice called out to Alexa to play Toni Braxton's latest song, 'Dance.' She stood up and began to dance, moving her hips left to right in front of Desmond. She held her hand out to him.

13

"Dance with me."

With no hesitation, Desmond stood. He pulled her closer to his body and rested his hands on her backside as they moved to the beat.

Candice caressed his face with her hands before bringing his head down to her. She softly brushed her lips against his. Desmond took her top lip into his mouth and sucked on it before inserting his tongue inside her mouth.

Candice broke the kiss, grabbed his hand, and led him down the hallway to her bedroom.

In her bedroom, she said, "Alexa, play Gotta Move on by Toni Braxton."

She pushed Desmond down onto the bed as she slowly undressed in front of him.

Desmond watched as he licked his lips. Once she finished, he stood and removed his clothes.

Candice dropped to her knees. She grabbed hold of his penis and ran her tongue alongside the head, and then across the head.

"Damn baby, don't do me like this," Desmond whispered.

Candice grabbed the base of his penis. She moved her hand slightly up and down as she licked the side of his penis. She licked him up and down before making him disappear into her mouth.

Candice and Desmond had been together a while before he told her about his wife, but Candice already knew about her from her friend Karen.

Monday evening, after dinner, Candice and Desmond retired to the bedroom.

Candice was lying down on her back as Desmond made love to her body. Desmond started from the bottom of her feet. He moved his way up her body as he kissed and caressed every inch of her.

14

He came to her breasts. He ran his tongue over her nipple and circled it before taking it into his mouth. He moved between her legs, and grabbed hold of his manhood, and inserted himself. His strokes were slow at first, and then he went deeper. He rolled over as he pulled Candice on top of him. She rode him and matched him stroke for stroke as they became faster and faster, and then his cell phone rang. They both looked over at his phone as she remained on top of him. She continued to move up and down harder and faster.

"Don't you dare reach over for that phone, and it better not be that bitch wife of yours."

Desmond screamed from the pleasure, "Fuck, aw shit. I have to. It's Stephanie. It could be an emergency."

After he released himself, he rolled over and grabbed his phone off the nightstand. Candice stared at him in disbelief.

"As I said, I have to call her back. It could be an emergency."

"That bitch is going to be a thorn in my side?"

Desmond looked at Candice sideways as she got up and walked into the restroom.

"That bitch still happens to be my wife!"

Desmond yelled loud enough for Candice to hear.

"Not for long if I can help it." Candice said softly under her breath.

CHAPTER 2

Desmond Taylor, a graduate of Harvard law. A Junior attorney at one of the largest law firms in the world, Kirkland and Ellis. Desmond and his wife Stephanie had been married for ten years. During the ten years, Stephanie Taylor, an African American female who gave up her dreams of becoming a nurse. So she could help support her husband through law school. She and Desmond had a good life. Everything seemed to be going like Stephanie had always dreamed of except for being able to give Desmond a child.

One month later
Stephanie was asleep by the time Desmond walked through the door. He tiptoed into their bedroom, careful not to wake her. He removed his clothes and quietly slipped into bed.
The ringing of the alarm awoke Stephanie. She looked over at her husband, who appeared to be sleeping so peacefully. She shut the alarm off, sat up on the side of the bed, and yawned. She dragged herself out of bed and into the kitchen to make breakfast for her husband.
The bacon was frying, and the toast in the toaster had just popped up. Stephanie stood as she whipped eggs. Desmond walked into the kitchen. Stephanie turned when she heard the refrigerator door open.
    "Oh, so we can't speak this morning? You have been coming home late every night this week. If I did not know any better, I would say you're…"
Desmond cuts her off, "Stephanie, I am not trying to argue with you this morning."
    "It is apparent that you are not trying to do anything with me, Desmond."
    "And I am going to pass on breakfast this morning.

I have an early meeting."

Desmond grabbed a piece of toast and his briefcase.

"Desmond!" Stephanie called out.

"I am sorry, and I will be home late again tonight so don't wait up for me."

"Desmond, we need to talk."

"We will talk this weekend, I promise. There's something I need to talk with you about."

Stephanie stood there looking at Desmond's back as he walked out. For the last month, Desmond had been acting differently. They have not had sex in weeks, and now he even avoids kissing her. Her intuition told her something was up.

Stephanie grabbed her cell phone and phoned her manager. Stephanie had been a broker with Charles Schwab & Company for the last ten years

"Hey, Susan, I'm taking a PTO today. I need to handle some things."

Susan, a single black woman in her mid-40s. Stephanie's boss and best friend of nine years.

"Is everything okay? Susan asked.

"I am not sure, but I will let you know later. I am going to follow Mr. Taylor today. My gut tells me something is not right, so I'm going to find out."

Stephanie disconnected the call and hopped in the shower.

An hour later, "Mr. Taylor, you have a call on line one."

"Cynthia, hold all my calls for about an hour," Desmond said in between kisses.

"It's your wife."

"I said hold my calls!" Desmond yelled.

Cynthia rolled her eyes, "I'm sorry, Mrs. Taylor, but Mr. Taylor is in a meeting. I can have him call you when he gets out, if that's okay?"

"Thanks, but don't bother."

Stephanie sat outside her husband's office as she disconnected the call. Stephanie got out of her car and walked toward the office. She did not believe one bit that he was in a meeting. For the last month, this was the same excuse she got each time she called her husband. But today, she would find out what's behind his avoidance.

As she made her way inside the building, she waived at Tim at the guard's station. She made her way over to the elevator and rode up to the thirteenth floor.

As she stepped off the elevator and walked down the hallway, she saw her husband's secretary.

"Good morning, Cynthia."

Cynthia Smiled, "Good morning, Mrs. Taylor."

Cynthia, a middle-aged Hispanic female who had been with the firm for nine years.

Cynthia watched Mrs. Taylor and didn't stop her as she walked over to Desmond's office door. Stephanie slowly turned the knob, but it was locked. She looked back at Cynthia, who had the key in her hand.

"You did not get this from me," Cynthia said.

Stephanie winked at Cynthia as she moved back to the door. She put the key in and turned the knob slowly.

"Oh shit! This feels so damn good!" Desmond yelled.

He continued to pump her harder and harder.

Stephanie closed the door behind her. She walked further into the room, "You better get used to that dick, because when I am finished with his ass, a dick will be all you're going to get."

Candice and Desmond jumped. Candice covered her breasts with her hands while Desmond pulled up his pants and ran toward Stephanie.

Stephanie turned her back and headed for the door.

"Stephanie, honey, I can explain!" Desmond said.

Stephanie turned around, "You can explain! What is there

18

to explain? Now I see why you have been acting differently. Coming home at all hours of the night smelling like cheap perfume. I will deal with yo ass at home!"

Desmond stood there with his pants unbuttoned. Candice put her blouse on, buttoned it up, and pulled her skirt down.

"Let her go. And besides, she was bound to find out about us eventually... seeing that I'm pregnant."

Desmond's head spun around.

"Whoa! How can that be? I used protection every single time."

Candice held up the pregnancy test and laughed.

"You know condoms aren't always 100% all the time. Maybe one of yours had a hole in it," Candice said. Desmond stared at her in disbelief and then he became angry. He walked up to her and pointed his finger in her face, "You can't keep this baby. I'm not doing this to my wife!"

"You're not doing this to your wife! Look at what you have been doing to her for all these months! I guess you really should have thought about that before you started fucking me, but I'm keeping this baby with or without you! Now it's your choice whether you want to be a part of it or not!?" Candice grabbed her purse, rolled her eyes as she walked past Desmond, and headed for the door.

"Candice, wait! We need to sit down and talk about this. I need time to think about this situation."

Candice stopped and turned around. Candice said with an attitude, "You can take all the time you want, but I am keeping our baby."

That evening, Desmond walked in and found Stephanie sitting on the couch watching TV and drinking a glass of wine. He laid his jacket and briefcase down.

"Can we talk?"

Stephanie looked over at him and said nothing.

"I never meant for this to happen. I wasn't out there

looking for this, it just happened, but she makes me feel wanted. She gets me. She supports me with my decisions, and she doesn't make me feel like I'm nothing."

Stephanie set her glass down, got up off the couch, and walked to stand directly in front of Desmond.

Stephanie laughed, "She supports you, really? Where was this bitch at when I put your narrow ass through Law School?" Stephanie pushed him in the chest with both hands.

"Where was she at when they were going to repo your fucking car, and I had to pawn my wedding rings to catch you up on your payments? Where was she when my family had to refinance their home, helping us keep our home? I gave up my dreams so you could have yours, and this is how you pay me back, you selfish son of a bitch!"

Stephanie slapped Desmond so loud the neighbor probably heard it. He grabbed the side of his face and looked at her.

"I'm so sorry Stephanie, I never meant to hurt you. If I could take this back, I would, but I can't, and now... we're expecting a baby."

Stephanie hit him. Desmond grabbed her arms and held her tightly.

" I hate you! How could you do this to me?"

"Stephanie, I am so sorry. I will be out by this weekend, and I'll have someone at the office draw up the divorce papers. I'll give you whatever you want."

Stephanie broke loose from Desmond and looked at him with tears in her eyes as she became angry again, "So you're going to leave me, just like that. I see because she's white, she's right! You black men kill me with that bullshit. And then you label us as angry black women, I wonder why we are angry? But yo ass will regret this, Desmond, MARK MY FUCKIN WORDS!"

Stephanie walked over and cut off the television, grabbed her wine, and was heading upstairs, but she stopped and turned around to look at Desmond.

"You can get your shit out tonight. Leave my key on the kitchen table, and if your shit is still here tomorrow when I wake up, I will do a Waiting to Exhale on yo ass."

CHAPTER 3

Jason Santiago and Desmond had been best friends since childhood. Jason was the color of bronze, tall and very handsome with hazel eyes and jet-black wavy hair. He is every woman's wet dream. He's a fitness instructor and owns three gyms. He's a bachelor and is looking for someone to settle down with, someone that has the same qualities as Stephanie.

"Man, I can't believe you did this to my girl. Stephanie is every man's dream. What were you thinking?" Jason asked.

"I wasn't. And the funny thing is, I was going to call it off with Candice this weekend before we got caught and before I found out she was pregnant."

"So are you going to marry her?"

"Yeah, I don't want any man playing daddy to my child."

"You have got to be kidding! Do you even love her? If you marry her, don't expect me to be at the wedding."

"What! You wouldn't be my best man?"

"Hell to the naw! I can't do it. Stephanie is my girl. I can't disrespect her like that."

"Jason, we have been friends since kindergarten. How can you choose Stephanie over me? And the answer to your question, I love her, but I'm not in love with her, yet."

"Yet, and no I'm not choosing one over the other. I want to respect you both, and for me to do that, I can't be a part of your wedding." Jason said.
Jason shook his head.

"I can't believe you are giving up everything to be with a woman who you're not in love with? Oh, my God! The sex must be real good."

The ringing of the phone awoke Stephanie. She reached over and grabbed it. She looked over for Desmond and then remembered what happened last night.

"Hello."

"Hey girl, are you coming in today so we can talk?" Susan asked.

Stephanie whispered, "He's divorcing me for a white woman."

"What!"

"Yep, you heard me right."

"Stephanie, I am so sorry to hear that. Do you need to take some time off?"

"I do need to keep myself busy. Maybe I could take a couple of days off and get my office set up since I will be going back to school online in the evening."

"Good for you. How about I stop by this evening and bring dinner?"

"That sounds good."

"Okay, I will see you then."

After talking with Stephanie, Susan walked down the hall to speak with Karen. She knocked at Karen's door.

"Are you busy?"

"No, come on in." Susan shut the door behind her.

Desmond called Cynthia on the phone, "Cynthia can you come into my office."

Cynthia walked into Desmond's office.

"Shut the door behind you."

Cynthia took a seat in front of Desmond.

"Yesterday, my office door was locked, but my wife was still able to get inside. Do you know anything about that?"

"No, I was actually on the phone when she stepped off the elevator. I thought you let her in, and by the time I got off my call, I saw her leaving"

23

"Are you sure?"

"Yes. Did something happen?"

Desmond eyed her suspiciously. He knew how much Cynthia adored Stephanie. He wouldn't put it pass Cynthia if she called and told Stephanie about him and Candice.

"No, everything's good. You're excused."

Cynthia walked out with a smile on her face. She was so glad his ass got caught.

Cynthia was married for 15 years when her husband decided he wanted someone younger. He left her and her three kids without anything. She lost all respect for Desmond once she learned what was going on with him and Candice.

Stephanie was in Desmond's office as she packed his belongings. She slammed his certificates and shattered the glass as she threw them into the box when the tears started to fall.

She picked up a picture of her and Desmond and sent it flying across the wall.

"I hate this motherfucker! I lost two babies behind his ass. I was stressed out working two jobs, putting his ass through law school. Now that he's doing good, he cheats on me with that piece of trash because she can give him something that I can't. Desmond, you and that bitch can go straight to hell!"

Just then, the doorbell rang. Stephanie wiped her eyes. She took her time answering the door, and when she did, she got a surprise.

"Oh my God!"

A man was hiding behind two dozen red and white roses. Stephanie reached for the vase, and there stood her husband's best friend. Her smile turned into a frown.

Jason noticed it quickly, "Sorry! I didn't mean to disappoint you." Jason said.

"I am sorry Jason. I just thought you were Desmond. Thank you and you shouldn't have. What are you doing here?"

"Do I have to have a reason to come see you?"

"No, come on in, and I guess you already heard what happened."

"Yep, that's why I am here. Are you okay?"

"I'm numb right now. I can't believe Desmond would do this to me. It just seems like a bad dream."

"Would you ever consider taking him back?"

Jason moved further inside the home. Stephanie looked at Jason as she placed the vase with the roses on one of her end tables.

"I would have last night, but after thinking about the situation, no, I can't do it, especially since he cheated with a white woman."

"Well, so you know, Desmond spent the night with me."

"So he didn't stay with his bitch?"

Jason laughed and shook his head.

"No."

"Well, while you're here, can you take some of his things with you to give to him? I told him last night that if I found his stuff still here; I was going to do a Waiting to Exhale on him, but I don't even have the energy to do that."

"Damn, remind me never to make you mad."

Jason stepped over the broken picture frame as he walked into the office. He watched Stephanie as she looked around the office. Then it hit her again, and the tears began to fall. Jason walked over to Stephanie and pulled her to him, and with one hand, he held her head against his chest.

"Stephanie, get it all out. I want you to know everything will be okay. I'm here for you sweetheart."

Jason's heart ached for Stephanie.

Stephanie looked up at Jason.

"Jason, I can't believe he would do this to me. If he

wasn't happy, why didn't he come and talk to me?"

"I know, Stephanie. I felt the exact way when Robin cheated on me. I gave her everything, but I guess that wasn't enough. Now you see why it's been hard for me to trust again."

Jason stepped back from Stephanie.

"I hate to leave you like this, but I have to get out of here. Is there anything else you need help with before I leave?"

"No, that's it."

"Would you mind if I pray with you before I leave?"

"No."

Jason grabbed her hands and bowed his head.

"Father, in the name of Jesus, I come to you and ask that you comfort Stephanie, give her peace and clarity. Heal her broken heart and let her know that Desmond's action had nothing to do with her. Father, I ask that you keep her safe in your arms and that each day you give her the strength to move on. In Jesus name. Amen."

Stephanie cried, "That was so sweet, Jason. I'm so glad to have you as a friend, and I hope Desmond and my situation doesn't change that."

Jason wiped away Stephanie's tears with his finger.

"Never, and he knows that."

"Well let me walk you to the door, and again, thank you for everything."

Jason kissed Stephanie on the forehead and left.

Desmond sat outside the house in his car and saw Jason walking out the door.

"What the hell!"

Desmond got out of the car and ran over to Jason as he was putting Desmond's belonging in the back seat.

"Hey man, why are you here! Desmond yelled."

Jason looked up at Desmond. "Uh, I stopped by to see how

Stephanie was doing."

"Oh, so you're sniffing around my wife now?"

"Come on Desmond, man, I'm not doing this with you? I told you, I would remain friends with both of you. Oh, and while you're here, take the rest of your things."

Jason shoved the box into his chest, got in his car, and took off as Desmond stood holding the box.

CHAPTER 4

A tall, dark, and handsome man who resembled Morris Chestnut dressed in tan khakis approached the table where Candice sat patiently waiting. Rodney had committed more murders than you can count before they arrested him, but there was no evidence to prove it on this one particular murder.

Rodney smiled, "Damn, don't you look good!"

Candice looked up, stood, and walked into Rodney's opened arms.

"Hey baby, how are you? Did you get the money I sent you?"

"Yes, I did, and thank you."

Rodney sat down, holding Candice's hand, looking at her up and down.

"So, how are the plans coming along?"

"I got the ball rolling. I told him I was pregnant, and he believed it. You must thank your sister for the pregnancy test, and we need to thank Karen for the information about Desmond."

"I can do that, but don't lose focus, okay. Don't fall in love with this dude."

"Oh, never that."

"So when are you going to tell him about my case?"

"Once we get our new place, I will casually bring it up. I am going to tell Desmond you are my cousin Trina's man. I will put all the details in one of my letters, and I will send it to you so you will know what's up when he meets with you."

"How do you know he will do it?"

"He wants to make a name for himself. I did my homework just like you told me to."

"Good girl, but you know once Carlos and his men find

out about my case being reopened, there might be trouble."

"Well, we will cross that bridge when we come to it."

Desmond phoned Candice.

"I just checked into the JW downtown. My room number is 1315. How long will it take you to get here?" Desmond asked.

"I'm Forty-five minutes outside of Indianapolis, so it may take me a while to get there, but I will be there," Candice said.

Stephanie and Susan sat around the fireplace, eating Chinese food with a bottle of wine.

"So how are you really feeling?"

"I'm okay right now, I think I have cried all I can cry. I just never thought Desmond and I would get to this point."

"Neither did I. I thought you guys were the perfect couple." Susan smiled.

"He broke my heart, but why? What did I do or didn't do? I did all I knew to do. He told me she didn't make him feel like he was nothing. How did I make him feel that way?"

"Sometimes men try to make us feel like we did something wrong, so they can feel good about what they are doing. But sometimes we're not as good as we think we are."

Stephanie glared at Susan.

"I'm not talking about you. I know you were good to Desmond." Susan rolled her eyes as Stephanie looked away.

"I guess that's why he said he would give me anything I wanted in the divorce."

Candice stepped out of the shower as Desmond laid in bed waiting.

29

"God! You are so beautiful!" Desmond said.

Desmond looked up at Candice as she stood on the side of the bed.

Candice looked down at Desmond. "More beautiful than your wife?"

"Candice, let's not go there."

"You're not having second thoughts, are you? Are you sure this is what you want?"

"I'm here, aren't I?"

"Your wife caught us making love, and if that hadn't happened, would you be getting a divorce?"

Candice slid in bed right next to Desmond.

"Shh, enough talking."

Desmond climbed on top of Candice and kissed his way down her body.

The next day, Stephanie's doorbell rang. Stephanie pulled the covers over her head. She was exhausted. She had been up all night crying. The doorbell rang again and again.

"Dammit, who is it!"

Stephanie made her way to the door and opened it.

"Good morning. I wanted to drop some coffee and bagels off before I head into work this morning."

"Jason, you didn't have to do this, I'm good."

Jason looked at Stephanie. He could tell she had been crying.

"Your eyes tell a different story."

Stephanie gave Jason a look.

"Just saying. I'm not staying, I wanted to drop these items off."

Jason walked down the walkway to his car.

"Thank you!" Stephanie yelled.

Jason waved his hand. "Call me if you need anything." He said without looking back.

Desmond sat in a meeting with a potential client.

"They arrested my brother on a murder charge last night, and we all know they framed him."

"And how do you know they framed him?"

"He was scheduled to testify against some big drug dealer, and now he's being framed."

"What's your brother's name, and where is he being held?"

"He's still in lockup, and his name is Antonio Martinez."

"I'll check into his case, and I will get back to you. If I decide to handle his case, I will need a fifty thousand dollar retainer."

"What! Where am I going to get that kind of money from?"

"Well, if money is an issue, your brother should look into getting a public defender. You came to the largest law firm in the United States. What did you expect?" He said sarcastically.

 The client stood up and rolled her eyes.

Desmond leaned back in his chair and smiled.

"I'm just being honest with you, it's company policy, and you know I don't make the rules around here."

CHAPTER 5

"**H**ey Stephanie, how are you? You know, it surprised me when I saw your file come across my desk." Jessica Stewart Divorce Attorney said.

"You're no more surprised than I am."

"Here, have a seat and tell me what's going on."

"He wants a divorce."

"What happened, and what do you want?"

"He cheated, and now he wants a divorce. I want everything. I want half of his 401K and retirement. I want him to pay for me to go back to school, and I want the house. I want his name off of it."

Kirland and Ellis

Stephanie walked up to Cynthia's desk. "Hey Cynthia, is Desmond available?"

"Good Afternoon, Mrs. Taylor. He's with a client, but you're welcome to have a seat and wait. He shouldn't be too much longer."

"Thanks."

"Can I get you anything?" Cynthia asked.

"Thanks, but no, I'm good, and by the way, I wanted to thank you for the other day." Stephanie said as she placed the key back in her hand.

Desmond walked the client out and saw Stephanie. Stephanie stood. "Can I have a word with you?"

"Sure, come right in."

Inside his office, Desmond took a seat behind his desk.

"Have a seat. I'm surprised to see you."

"I just left my attorney's office."

She tossed the folder on his desk.

"I asked for everything. I want half of your retirement and your 401K, the house, and for you to pay for me to go back to school."

"You don't want much, do you?"

"I want what I deserve. I was good to you and very supportive, and for you to do this to me, it's fucked up, and you know it. I don't know why you said I made you feel like nothing. You made yourself feel like that, not me. I only encouraged you, I never tore you down no matter how wrong I thought you were."

"Is that how you see it."

Stephanie stood. "Bitch, yes, that's how I see it!"

Desmond sat with a smirk on his face.

"Okay, well, since you've said what you came to say, let this be the last time you visit my office."

Stephanie rolled her eyes and walked out of the office, slamming the door back against the wall. Cynthia and two of the partners were there and looked up as she walked past them as the tears rolled down her face.

"That son-of-a-bitch was so smug. I could have slapped that smirk right off his face."

"What is up with him? I've never known him to act like this," Susan asked.

"What do you mean, you've never known him to act like this?"

"Oh, uh, I mean, you never said anything to me about him acting like that. You've always had good things to say about him."

"It's that bitch, Candice. He thinks he's all that since he has her on his arm. He better realize GOD don't like ugly."

"Yeah, and he ain't too fond of cute either." She looked at Stephanie.

"Oh, I almost forgot the reason I came here. I need the number for that handyman you use. I need some work done around the house."

"Sorry, but I stopped dealing with him a month ago when I caught him stealing some of my jewelry. Why don't you ask Jason? You know Jason would do anything for you."

Later that evening, Stephanie opened the door to let Jason in.

"I hope you didn't have any plans this evening, but I wanted to get this work started as soon as possible.

"Even if I had plans, I would have canceled them," Jason said.

Stephanie ignored his remark and continued walking down the hall to her office.

"I went out and bought this ceiling fan this morning. The clerk said it included everything that I needed."

Jason looked at the back of the box.

"Yep, everything is in here."

"Well, I am going to be in the kitchen cooking. Yell if you need anything."

"I could use a glass of water."

"Okay, water coming up."

Jason removed his shirt and placed it on the back of the chair.

Stephanie returned with the glass of water.

"Here you go."

Stephanie looked Jason up and down, checking out his body, while Jason pretended not to notice as he smiled.

Forty five minutes later, Stephanie stood at the stove as she tasted her meat sauce when Jason walked in. He watched and admired her in silence as she prepared her meal. Jason moved further into the kitchen.

"All finished," Jason said as he eased up behind her.

Stephanie jumped.

Jason laughed, "I'm sorry, I didn't mean to scare you."

"That's okay."

"Damn, you got it smelling good in here."

"Would you like to stay for dinner? I don't want to eat alone this evening."

"Sure, but you will have to do me a favor."

"What kind of favor?"

"I have this business meeting Friday evening, I would like for you to attend with me, so I don't have to fight off the single ladies."

"Fight off the single ladies? You mean to tell me you don't enjoy all that attention."
Stephanie said as she handed him a plate of food.

"Not all attention is good attention. And you know, since Robin and I split up, it's been hard trusting and getting close to another woman." He looked directly into Stephanie's eyes.

"That's understandable," Stephanie said as she looked away.

"So, do we have a deal?"

"I guess I can help you out. What time on Friday, and what's the attire?"

"I will pick you up at 7, and it's a Black Tie attire."

Desmond laid across the bed as Candice looked out the hotel room window.

"How long are we going to be here?" Candice asked as she turned to look at Desmond.

"Not too much longer. I have a friend who is going to show me his condo he is leasing on Friday, and if I like it, we can move in immediately."

"Nice. Have you filed for your divorce yet?"

"I didn't have to. Stephanie beat me to it."

"Really, what does she want?"

"I rather not talk about that. What I want to talk about is the baby. When is the due date?"

"December 20th."

"Man, I hope it's a girl."

"Me too. Why don't you order us some food and then meet me in the shower." Candice changed the subject. She did this every time Desmond would mention the baby.

After ordering dinner, Desmond walked in and saw Candice awaiting his arrival. He took slow strides to her. As he eased inside, she moved toward him, reached down, and grabbed his manhood.

"Damn!"

Candice licked the head of his penis and circled it with the tip of her tongue. Desmond leaned back up against the wall of the shower as Candice made him disappear inside her mouth.

CHAPTER 6

Stephanie was in her office at Charles Schwab when Susan popped her head in.

"Good morning, and just so you know, Karen found out about you and Desmond."

"Does she ever stop? I thought once she got with Michael, she would be good, damn!" Stephanie said.

Karen, a white redhead with green eyes in her late forties. An average-looking short, dumpy female who has been a thorn in Stephanie's side since she started 15 years ago. Right before Stephanie met Desmond, she dated a person named Michael, who cheated on her with Karen. They have been at odds with each other since.

Stephanie was busy working when she heard a knock at her door. Stephanie looked up.

"What can I do for you Karen?" Stephanie asked with an attitude.

"I heard the news. I just wanted to check on you to make sure you're okay."

"And why would you care?" Stephanie asked, trying to stay calm.

"To be honest, I really don't care. I was trying to be nice."

Stephanie looked at her and laughed.

"Well, why don't you take your nice ass back to your office."

"I would have thought by now that you would have learned that black men don't like angry black women," Karen said.

"That's because they like ugly fat women like you!" Stephanie yelled as Karen walked away with her nose turned up.

"That pudgy bitch!"

Jason was training one of his female clients when Desmond walked up to him.

"Hey, can I have a minute of your time?"

"Tammy, continue with three more reps, and I will be right back."

Desmond and Jason walked over to the corner of the gym.

"What's up?"

"Why don't you tell me?"

"Hey, you came to talk to me. So you tell me what's up."

"I see you have still been sniffing around Stephanie?"

"What! Man, what are you talking about?"

"Were you there last night?"

"Yes, I was. I installed a ceiling fan in her new office, and she asked me to stay for dinner because she didn't want to eat alone."

"And you don't see anything wrong with that"

"No."

Desmond pointed his finger at Jason.

"I want you to stay away from her! Do you hear me?"

"Who the hell do you think you are coming on my job talking shit? Remember bro, you left Steph, she didn't leave you, so be fucking happy with your new life."

"You heard what I said, and stop calling her Steph!"

Desmond walked off.

Jason walked back over to his client.

"Go ahead with the next rep, and I will be right back."

Jason walked back into his office to get his phone.

Stephanie was sitting at her desk when Jason called.

"Hey Jason, what's going on?."

"I hate to bother you at work, but Desmond just left. I think he's been watching you. He knew I was at your place yesterday and told me to stay away."

"What! He has a lot of nerves."

"Exactly."

"Well, I say let's give him something else to be mad about. How about dinner tonight at my place? Let's say around 7?"

"Are you sure?"

"Definitely."

"Okay, I will be there. Do I need to bring anything?"

"How about some wine?"

As soon as Stephanie hanged up from Jason, she called Desmond.

"Hello, Stephanie."

"Did you sign the papers yet?"

"Why are you in such a hurry to get this over with?"

"I'm just ready to move on with the next chapter of my life. Oh, and just so you know, I can have anyone I want over here, is that clear?

"Yes, just as long as it is not my best friend."

"You know what, I will fuck your best friend if I want. You got a lot of nerves; you know that. And just for the record, Jason and I will have dinner again tonight, and if that leads to something else, so be it, so mind your fucking business!

Stephanie disconnected the call.

Forty minutes later, Mr. Chris, the head of HR, and Susan knocked on Stephanie's door.

"Come in."

The look on their faces told Stephanie something was wrong.

"Hey, what's going on?"

"I was hoping you could tell us," Mr. Chris said.

He tossed five folders on her desk. Stephanie looked through the folders. "What's going on with my clients?"

"We received calls from your clients about unauthorized transfers."

"Okay, so who did this?"

Susan and Mr. Chris sat there and looked directly at her.

"What? Do you think I have something to do with it?"

"Who else would do this? We know you're going through a divorce, and money might be an issue. We just wish you would have come to us with any issues."

Stephanie looked at Susan, who avoided eye contact with her.

"Susan, you know me better than anyone. You know I wouldn't do anything like this, and for the record, I may be going through a divorce, but believe me, honey," she said as she looked at Susan. "Money is not one of my issues."

"Well, until we can sort this out, we have to suspend you. We will need your office keys, and we need you to clear out your office," Mr. Chris said.

"Are you serious! I have worked my butt off for this company for the last 15 years, and you're firing me like that with no evidence?" Stephanie said.

Mr. Chris and Susan stood as security approached Stephanie's door.

Mr. Chris turned to leave.

"When you're finished, these guys will escort you out."

"Oh, so it's like that now?"

Stephanie shook her head as she watched them leave.

When Susan walked out, she had a smirk on her face that some of the employees noticed.

Stephanie packed her belongings into a box. She stopped, and looked at the security guards.

"What! What are you guys looking at? I'm not taking anything that doesn't belong to me!"

CHAPTER 7

"**I** can't believe this is happening."

"Well, there's something I should tell you about your friend Susan," Jason said.

"No, Jason. Don't tell me she has stabbed me in my back too."

" I hate to tell you this, but I think she and Desmond had a brief affair. He would never admit to it. But she showed up twice when we were at the club. They talked and danced the entire time."

"And you never said anything to me about it?

"He swore up and down that nothing was going on. I didn't want to stir up any trouble if he was telling the truth.

Susan and Karen sat in Susan's office.

"Well, our plan worked," Susan said.

"I can't believe they are so fucking stupid."
They both laughed.

"Let's toast to Stephanie. If it wasn't for her going through a divorce, our plan may not have worked."
Susan and Karen held up their bottled water and said in unison, "To Stephanie."

Stephanie was in the kitchen making dinner when the doorbell rang.
It surprised Stephanie when she opened the front door.

"What are you guys doing here?"
You know we had to come and check on you," Judy said."

"Yeah, once we heard they fired you, we knew something was not right."

"Come on in."

"Girl, that Susan ain't right. She and Karen have become buddies."

"Really. When did that happen?"

"They have been sneaking around together for about two weeks now."

"Yeah, and I can't believe Susan didn't warn you about what was going on? "

"Did you see the smirk on her face when she walked out of Stephanie's office?" Frank asked.

"What exactly happened?" Judy asked.

Stephanie sat in disbelief as she listened.

"Can I trust you guys?"

Frank rolled his neck. "Come on, Stephanie."

"The five big accounts that I brought in have had some fraudulent activities. And they think I have embezzled money from the accounts. But it could have been anyone. I'm not the only one that had access to the accounts. It's funny because they brought up me going through a divorce trying to make it appear I needed money."

"And who do you think brought that up?" Frank asked.

"My good ole best friend," Stephanie said.

"So how are we going to clear your name?" Frank asked.

Jason walked up the walkway and noticed two cars in the driveway.

The doorbell rang. "Excuse me. I will be right back."

Ten minutes later, everyone sat at the kitchen table eating dinner.

"I can't believe they accused you of embezzlement," Jason said.

"I could go to prison if I don't clear my name."

"Who all has access to your accounts?"

"My CSP, the processing team, and Susan."

"Don't forget, the managers can get access if they need it," Frank said.

"Yeah, like Karen," Judy said.

"What do you want us to do?" Frank asked.

"I need to find out where the funds went and who approved the transfers. With my accounts, there have to be two approvers."

"So basically, there are two people involved."

The next day, Susan and Karen were heading out to lunch, and as soon as they did, Frank and Judy went into action.

"Be the lookout and hum if you see anyone coming," Frank told Judy.

"Okay, and here is her user ID and password. Whatever you do, please do not leave this in her office." Judy said as she handed him the index card.

Judy sat at her desk, right across from Susan's office, being the lookout person.

Frank walked into Susan's office and shut the door behind him.

He logged onto her laptop and pulled up the five accounts to see where the funds in question went, and how much was transferred.

JPMorgan Chase Bank and Wells Fargo. "Okay, now let's see the account numbers," Frank said aloud.

Frank searched for a pen to jot down the account numbers. He opened two drawers before he found a pen.

Karen and Susan were in the lobby of the building when Susan searched her purse for her phone. "Damn, think I left my phone upstairs. Hold on. I will be right back."

Susan got on the elevator heading up to her office.

Judy was busy on the phone talking when she looked up to see Susan walking up.

"Sir, can you hold please?"

Judy hummed, but Frank didn't hear her, so she hummed a little louder.

Frank looked up to see Susan at the door. He shut the laptop and hid underneath the desk.

43

Susan walked in and saw her cell phone.

"There you are."

Susan grabbed her cell phone and was getting ready to sit behind her desk and check her messages.

Frank panicked. He thought she knew he was there. He closed his eyes as Susan walked toward the back of her desk.

Out of breath, Judy rushed over to Susan's office to stop her before she walked behind her desk.

"Susan, you have a visitor at the guard's desk downstairs."

Susan looked at Judy suspiciously.

"What, I was just down there," Susan said. She noticed how nervous Judy looked.

"Well, Lewis just called."

Susan walked out and shut her door.

Frank got up from under the desk, walked over, and looked out through the blinds. He eased out the door when he saw Susan hop on the elevator.

Frank walked over to Judy's desk and whispered. "Well, hell, do you know what a lookout person does? If I had gotten caught, I would have lost my job.

"I'm sorry, but I got a phone call. Did you find anything?"

"Yes, I did, but I didn't get the account numbers."

"That was a close call."

"No shit! Too close for me. I still need to get those account numbers. Maybe I'll stay a little late this evening."

Desmond and Candice arrived at the condo his friend was leasing.

"Hey Desmond, nice to see you. Oh, I was expecting you and your wife, Stephanie."

Roger gave Desmond a side-eye glance.

"Candice, this is Roger, a good friend from college."

"Nice to meet you, Roger," Candice said as she smiled.

"Okay, well, I will let you guys look around, and if you need anything, I will be right here."

Roger stepped outside to call his wife.

"Olivia, have you spoken to Stephanie lately?"

"No, why?"

"Desmond is here with a white woman."

"Well, maybe the condo is for her."

"Um… something doesn't seem right to me." He continued to talk with his wife, and a few minutes later, he heard Desmond calling out to him.

"Roger, Roger."

"I will call you back, they're calling me."

"Yes, what do you think?" Roger said as he walked back inside.

"We love it. We will take it."

"We?"

"Yes, we."

CHAPTER 8

Susan walked over to Frank's desk as he pretended to be busy.

"Working late, I see?"

"Yes, but I am getting ready to call it a night."

Frank realized Susan wasn't leaving anytime soon.

Susan walked to stand inside his cubicle and leaned up against it.

"Who was in my office while I was at lunch?"

"What are you talking about?"

"While I was out, someone was in my office on my laptop."

"Well, it wasn't me. I was working with Thomas."

"Are you sure, Frank?"

"I know what I was doing. And why would I lie?" Frank asked as he rolled his neck.

Friday evening rolled around and Stephanie had just finished getting dressed when Jason rang her doorbell. When Stephanie opened the door, Jason's mouth flew open, and his eyes bulged out.

"Is something wrong?" Stephanie asked

"No, not at all. I didn't expect you to look like this."

Stephanie smiled. "So, do you approve?"

Jason smiled. "Yes."

Jason and Stephanie arrived at the ballroom. They walked inside, and Stephanie looked over at Jason with a surprised look on her face.

"Oh my God! You didn't tell me this would be so elaborate."

"Yeah, they go all out for this event."

Jason and Stephanie walked around as he introduced her to

some of his friends. One friend stood out in particular. She remembered seeing her in Desmond's office one day. She eyed Stephanie suspiciously.

"Jason, who is the lady in the black mini dress that continues to look over here at us?"
He hesitated to answer. "She's a good friend of mine and Desmond."
She looked at him sideways. "How good of a friend?"
Jason pointed to the stage. An elegant lady in her early sixties, dressed in black and silver, walked on stage.

"Good evening, everyone, and thank you for joining us this year for our 10th year of celebrating Black Business Men. My name is Thelma Lewis, and I am one of the founders of this program. It thrills us to recognize the outstanding black businessmen here in our state. And this year, we will do something special for this individual. We know how hard you work, so we would like for you to take a weekend off on us and enjoy yourself. The winner of tonight's Top Black Business Man will win a paid trip for two to Gatlinburg, Tennessee, in one of the luxurious cabins Gatlinburg offers.
The crowd yelled and applauded.

"We've narrowed it down to five finalists. As I call your name please make your way to the stage."
Stephanie whispered into Jason's ear, "Are you one of the nominees?"
"Yes."
"Jason, why didn't you tell me?"
Stephanie looked at Jason and crossed her fingers.
Thelma opened the white envelope.

"Christopher Johnson, James Madrid, Michael Kirkland, Paul White, and last but not least, Jason Santiago."
Stephanie screamed and clapped.
"Yes!" Stephanie yelled.
Jason hugged Stephanie before he headed to the stage.

The crowd applauded the men on stage.

"We know you guys have worked so hard this year; we have a little something for you all."

Thelma turned around and handed each man a plaque with their name embroidered on it.

"How can I say this without giving away his name? Before I tell you a little about him? The winner is the owner of three facilities that help people get and stay in shape."

The crowd applauded, knowing Jason was the owner of three popular gyms.

"Well hell, you already know who he is. Congratulations Jason Santiago for being the top Black Business Man of 2020."

Thelma handed Jason the package for the cabin trip as he approached the podium to speak.

"Thank you very much. It feels awesome to receive an award for doing what you love to do on a day-to-day basis."

Jason looked back at Thelma. "I would like to thank Thelma for hosting this event every year and for the Top Black business Men program."

Twenty minutes later, the crowd mingled with one another as the music played softly in the background.

Stephanie smiled. "Congrats! Mr. Top Black Businessman of 2020."

"Thank you and thank you for agreeing to come with me."

Marsha, the lady dress in black that had eyed Jason and Stephanie since they walked in. She watched their every move. Just then, Marsha walked up to Jason and Stephanie. Marsha hugged Jason and congratulated him.

"Hey Jason, now that you have won that trip, you can take me away for the weekend." Stephanie looked over at the lady with a grin on her face.

"Hey, aren't you Desmond Taylor's wife?"

"Yes, I am."

"So why are you here with Jason?"

Jason eyed the lady.

Stephanie spoke before Jason had a chance to, "I don't think that's any of your business."

"She's minding her business. Like you should mind yours." Jason said.

Jason looked over at Stephanie. "Hey, let's get out of here."

Jason and Stephanie stood outside and waited for the valet to bring Jason's car around.

"Uh... You sure handled that lady."

"I liked the way you handled her better. She has no right to question any female that she sees me with."

The next day, Desmond ran out for coffee and bagels. He sat at a red light as he looked at his notifications on his phone. One notification in particular caught his attention. Mr. Top Businessman of 2020!

"Wow!"

Desmond continued to read as he scrolled down and read who the winner was.

"Um... Jason Santiago."

And then he saw the picture, the picture of Jason and Stephanie.

"Stephanie! Ah! What the fuck! My wife parading around town on his arm like arm candy all in my face for everyone to see! At least I did my shit behind closed doors."

Desmond sat there confused, and then it turned into rage as he looked at Stephanie with his best friend.

Desmond hit his steering wheel. He pulled off and made a U-turn, and instead of going home, he pulled into the parking lot of the gym. He checked Jason's office, but he was not there, so he went out on the floor where he saw Jason talking to a female.

Desmond interrupted their conversation.

"Can I have a word with you!" Desmond said with anger in his tone. Jason held his finger up to the female.

"Give me one second."

Jason walked toward the door, and Desmond followed him outside.

"What's up?" Jason asked.

Desmond threw a punch that caught Jason in the jaw. Jason grabbed his jaw.

"I thought I told you to say away from my wife!"

"Hell naw! You gon sucker punch me!"

Jason ran over and grabbed Desmond by both legs. He picked him up and slammed him down on top of his car.

Some of Jason's workers inside the gym heard the commotion and ran outside. They got in between the men.

"I don't know what your problem is, but if you come up to my job again, I promise I will fix it."

Jason yelled as he tried to get at Desmond, but his employees blocked his path.

"You fucking my wife is my problem!"

"I am not fucking her. We are friends like I thought we were. Don't get mad at me because you switched out your dime for a penny! That was all your doing! Jason looked him dead in his eyes.

"Regardless if y'all sleeping together or not, she is still my wife, so stay the hell away from her!"

"Man, go home to your fuckin penny!"

Jason moved one of his employees out of the way and walked inside to his office.

CHAPTER 9

Candice was busy unpacking things while Desmond was out when she came across a folder. She opened the folder, and there it was: the divorce papers.
She held the folder in her hands as she began to think. Candice folded the folder, and walked into their bedroom, and placed the folder inside her purse.

Stephanie was busy in her office signing up for some classes when she heard the doorbell ring. She laid her glasses down as she got up from her desk and walked to the front door.
She opened the door to find Desmond standing there.
"What do you want, Desmond?"
"How about you tell me what's going on with you and Jason? How bout that!"
Stephanie laughed and shook her head.
"That white girl got you all fucked up if you think you can come over here and question me about what I'm doing!"
"You know you are still my wife, right? And it doesn't look good for you going out with my best friend."
"I don't give a flying fuck how it looks. Again, what I do and who I do it with is my business like you leaving me for that white bitch, is your business. Now, what looks worse, huh, Desmond? Like I said, if I want to fuck Jason on the front lawn and slob all over his dick, that's my business. And now that we got that straight, there's no need for you to come over here anymore!"
Stephanie slammed the door in his face as he jumped back, just in time.
Stephanie was so angry; she leaned up against the front door and slid down to the floor as the tears fell. She cried

uncontrollably. "God, why? What did I do wrong? Why are you punishing me?"

Later that evening, Stephanie sat in the dark in her living room with a bottle of patron as she listened to Mary J. Blige. She had almost drunk half the bottle when she faintly heard the doorbell.

Stephanie staggered over to the front door and yelled.

"I thought I told you not to come back!"

Stephanie opened the front door to find Jason standing there. He got a good whiff of her breath.

"Jesus, Stephanie, are you drunk?"

Stephanie slurred her words.

"Drunk! Do I look drunk, man?"

And then she did the unthinkable. She vomited all over Jason's shirt and shoes. Stephanie looked down at Jason's shirts. She laughed, and then she burst out crying.

"Jason, I am so sorry! I don't know what's wrong with me."

She followed behind Jason as he made his way to the kitchen sink. He grabbed a roll of paper towels and removed his shirt.

"Oh my, Jason, you got muscles."

Stephanie started to laugh as she moved closer to Jason and touched his chest.

"Jason, Can I ask you a question?"

Jason looked down at her.

"Why are you still single?"

And then she vomited on her pajama top and bottoms.

"Oh my God! I don't feel so well Jason."

She started to unbutton her top, but Jason quickly stopped her.

"No, Steph!"

He guided her down the hall to the restroom.

Jason turned on the shower.

"Get in and leave your clothes on the floor. I will put

them in the washer."

Jason turned his back as she undressed and got inside the shower.

"I'm in."

Jason turned slowly, and bent down to get her clothes. He looked at her silhouette through the fogged glass doors. He stood there for a minute and ran his hand through his hair before leaving out.

Once Stephanie showered and was dressed for bed, Jason tucked her in.

"I don't want to leave you like this. Would it be okay if I crashed here tonight?"

"Sure. You know where the spare bedroom is. Make yourself comfortable."

"Do you need anything?"

"Yes, I have a headache. I have some Tylenol in the medicine cabinet."

Jason walked back in with two Tylenol's and a glass of water. He stood as she took the medicine, and then he set the glass on the nightstand. He bent down and kissed her on the forehead. Jason made his way to the living room and turned the television on.

The next morning, Stephanie awoke. She put her hand to her head. She appeared to be thinking, then sniffed the air and smelled coffee, and then she heard movement. She slowly got up and made her way to the kitchen.

Jason heard some noise and turned around.

"Well, good morning, and this time, say it don't spray it!"

Stephanie laughed slightly.

"I'm sorry about that. I am quite embarrassed. If Desmond had returned, that would've been perfect!"

"Oh, he ran up on you too yesterday?"

"Yes," Stephanie said.

53

"He got me first thing yesterday morning at the gym. We had an altercation outside."

"Are you serious? Stephanie laughed.

Jason looked at her with a confused look.

"What's funny?"

"Don't get upset, but I told him if I wanted to fuck you out on the front lawn, that it was my business."

"No you didn't."

"Yes I did. Who is he to tell me who I can see or not see?"

"Oh my God! I know he was livid. Jason shook his head and laughed. Anyway, do you feel better?"

"Yes, and thank you for looking after me, I appreciate it."

"I know the hurt you're feeling, and I'm glad you're letting it out in a safe place, but please lighten up on the drinking. Why don't you come down to the gym and take your hurt and frustration out on a punching bag?"

"Right!" Stephanie said.

They both laughed.

"Thanks for the laugh, but I gotta get dressed before my parents' get here, and since I don't feel like cooking, I need to think of somewhere to take them for brunch. Maybe I'll be able to hold something down by then."

"Ok, that's my cue to go."

Jason kissed Stephanie on the forehead and left.

An hour later, Stephanie pulled into the parking lot of the restaurant. She looked into the flipped-down mirror and applied lipstick to her lips, and she checked to see if she needed any more eye drops before getting out of the car.

"No more crying." She said as she walked toward the restaurant.

Stephanie whispered under her breath, "No bad news until the end."

Stephanie saw her parents walking hand in hand as they

approached the entrance, and they saw her and smiled. Her mother walked in, and her father held the door open for her as he scanned the parking lot for Desmond.

Stephanie hugged her mom as her mom spoke with the hostess.

"Is Desmond joining us?" Her dad asked.

"Party of three?" The hostess asked.

"Yes," Stephanie said.

"Follow me."

Walking to the table Stephanie laughed.

"No dad, he won't be joining us. I have you two all to myself."

CHAPTER 10

Jason was working in his office when Marsha showed up.

"So, what's up with you and Desmond's wife?" Marsha asked.

"Well, hello to you too!"

She stared at Jason, waiting on a response.

"What's it to you?"

"Does Desmond know you took his wife to the event?"

"Again, what is it to you? Marsha, I am busy, I don't have time for this."

"You had time for this last weekend... so what's changed."

She unbuttoned her blouse.

"Me!"

Jason stood and walked over to her and started buttoning up her blouse.

"You need to leave." He pointed to the door.

Stephanie and her parents' had just finished eating.

"You know your sister is expecting another baby."

"Really! Oh my God! That's what she wanted to tell me. I forgot to call her back." Stephanie rolled her eyes. Stephanie and her sister have always been at odds with each other. Sophia was the judgemental one. The one that never did any wrong in her parents' eyes. Stephanie on the other hand, had made too many mistakes according to her parents. She had always compared her to Sophia, which caused animosity between the sisters.

"You seem to be holding up pretty well considering the mess that's going on at your job." Her mom said.

"I'm doing the best I can. I don't know how they have a case against me when I'm not the only one with access to those accounts."

"Is Desmond going to handle the case for you?"

"No mom."

"Your dad and I were just saying we're glad you have Desmond to lean on for emotional and financial support."
Stephanie looked the other way. She didn't want to make eye contact with her mom.

"Exactly, and that's why it puzzles me he's not here this morning. The way that rascal loves breakfast. He started this brunch tradition with us years ago and never missed a beat, and today of all days he's distracted with what? What could be so distracting?"
Stephanie hesitated, her eyes watered. She decided to get it out.

"How about a mistress and a baby on the way!"
She looked at her dad as she laid the credit card on the table.
It shocked her parents.

"Stephanie, are you serious?"

"That muther."

"James!" Her mother put her hand on her husband's arm.

"Baby, why didn't you tell us."

"He moved out last week. He told me he wanted a divorce."

"I can't believe him. After all the shit he put you through and how you supported his ass!"

Monday morning, Frank sent Judy a message. Meet me on the third floor by the vending machines.
Judy took the elevator down to the third floor. As she got off the elevator, she saw Frank leaned up against the pop machine.

"I already know you saw the pics, right?"

"Um, hmm. Girl, that nigga is fine! She didn't waste any time, did she? They look good together, I'll give them that."

"Don't jump to conclusions. They could be just friends like they say they are."

"Right," Frank said.

"Now what about this fraud issue? I smell a rat, and HR needs to make sure they lay some traps out." Judy said.

"Or send out some cats," Frank said.
Judy's with narrow eyes, nodded her head with a devilish look.

"Now ya talking!"

"I wasn't able to get those account numbers on Friday. Don't you know the big bear worked late with me and had the nerve to ask me who was in her office while she was at lunch. How did she know?"

"You never gave me that index card back. Did you leave it in there?"

"Aw shit! I forgot!"

"I told you to make sure you gave that back to me. That's how she knows. Let's stay late this evening to see if I can get it."

"Okay, but I can't work too late. I got a hot date, and I don't want to keep my boo thang waiting." Frank rolled his neck and popped his tongue.

That evening, Frank and Judy waited until everyone had left.

"Damn! I didn't think she would ever leave with her ole nosey ass."
Just then his phone rang.

"Hold on, this is my sister. Hey girl, what's up?"

"Frank, I need a favor. I am in a bind right now. I have to work overtime and I need someone to pick Linda up from aftercare and bring her home," Tracy said.

"Tracy, you can't find anyone else to do it."

"If I could, I wouldn't have called you. Come on Frank, you know how aftercare is when you're late.

"Geez, I'm on my way, but you owe me big time."
Frank disconnected the call and looked at Judy with sad eyes.

"I hate to do this to you, but I have to go. My sister needs me to pick my niece up at aftercare. I'm sorry!"

"Don't worry! I got this," Judy said.

"Okay, but be careful."

After Frank left, Judy unlocked Susan's office. She walked behind her desk and sat down. She pulled up the accounts on her laptop and jotted down the account numbers.

"This was too easy," Judy said to herself.
Susan's door opened, and Judy looked up to see Karen. Judy closed the laptop.

"What do you want?"

"I should ask you that question? Does Susan know you're on her laptop?"
Judy stood and moved from behind the desk.

"Yes she does. I'm working on something for her."

"If I call her will she corroborate your story?"
Karen moved behind the desk and opened the laptop, and saw the bank account numbers. She looked back up at Judy and smiled. She took the black gloves from her purse.

"You're too nosey for your own good. You know that, right?"

"Whatever," Judy said as she walked out of the office. She turned off her computer, locked her credenza, and grabbed her purse. She stood by the elevator when suddenly someone came from behind her and everything went black.

CHAPTER 11

F**rank** looked up from his computer to see Susan standing there. "Have you heard from Judy this morning?"

"No, why?"

"She's not here, and she hasn't called in."

"Have you called her?"

"Yes, but she is not answering."

"Um... Let me call her, and I will let you know what's going on."

"Thanks, Frank."

As Susan walked away, Frank dialed Judy's number.

It rang four times, "Hey, how are you? Hold on while I turn the TV down, sike, I got you. Please leave a message, and I will return your call as soon as I can."

"Girl, you and that damn voice message. What's up with the no-call and no-show. Call your boss and then me ASAP!"

Rodney walked out grinning from ear to ear.

"Hey doll, how are you?"

Rodney hugged and kissed Candice.

"Hey babe. How's everything? I mailed you a letter on Friday with all the details so you should get it tomorrow."

"Cool. How was the move?"

"Not bad at all."

"How long do I have to wait for my new attorney?"

"Let me get engaged first. I will do whatever I can to speed up the divorce, and once I'm engaged, I will tell him about your sad story."

"What if he doesn't bite?"

"Trust me. I know how to convince him to do anything. We have a new condo together, don't we?"

"Don't let this backfire on us," Rodney said as he

looked Candice dead in her eyes.

"Let me handle this my way. If you had listened to me in the first place, you wouldn't even be in here."

"I guess you're right."

Stephanie was in her office registering for some classes when she got a call from Susan.

"Hello Stephanie, how are you?"

"What do you want?"

"We would like to meet with you tomorrow at 9 am."

"For what?"

"Some members from HR would like to speak with you."

"Should I bring my attorney?"

Susan hesitated. "Yes."

After hanging up from Susan, Stephanie panicked.

"What if they arrest me!" She said aloud. She was almost in tears, and then she thought about Jason.

"Maybe Jason can help me."

Stephanie dialed Jason's number. He picked up on the fourth ring.

"Jason, I need a favor!" Stephanie yelled.

"Whoa, whoa, whoa, calm down. What's wrong?"

"Susan just called me, and she said that HR wants me to come to the office tomorrow at 9 am for a meeting. I need a good attorney. Any suggestions. I just know they are going to arrest me!"

"They are not going to arrest you. Well, I guess Desmond is out of the question?" He laughed. "I'm sorry I shouldn't have said that, but I have a buddy who's a defense attorney. Let me call him, and I will call you right back."

"Thanks Jason."

The next day, Stephanie walked inside the building and took the elevator up to the Sixteenth floor. She was nervous

61

because the attorney nor Jason had called her back.

She had no idea what to expect. As she stepped off the elevator, all eyes were on her. As she walked down the hall to the conference room, a tall handsome man stood as she approached.

"You must be Stephanie."

"Yes, and you are?"

"I'm Todd Ransom. Jason's friend."

"Oh my God! Thank you for coming!"

"Jason has already filled me in. Is there anything you want to tell me?"

"I'm innocent. I would never embezzle money from anyone."

"That's exactly what I wanted to hear."

As the two stood talking, Karen walked past and saw Stephanie. She walked over to Frank's desk. "Has your girlfriend showed up yet?"

Frank looked at Karen and rolled his eyes as Karen started to walk away.

"I heard you say you worked late on Monday. Judy worked late also, so that makes you the last person to have seen her."

Karen turned back around. "Yes I did, but she left about 10 minutes before I did."

Frank saw Stephanie and her attorney walk into the conference room.

"That's too bad about your friend. I never took her for a thief," Karen said.

"And that's because she's not one. Why would an attorney's wife need to steal, and besides, she made damn good money here? Now I could think of some other people here that need money, especially when you have a man who doesn't work and depends on his stupid girlfriend."

"I know you're not talking about me!"

"Now why would I. Does the shoe fit?"

62

Karen rolled her eyes and walked off.

Frank smiled. "I guess she'll know the next time, bitch!"

Franks rolled his neck and snapped his fingers. His co-workers burst out laughing.

As Stephanie and her attorney walked inside, they were greeted by two police officers, Susan, and four men from HR. The senior HR person, Mr. Chris, pointed at the two chairs for Stephanie and her attorney to sit.

"Stephanie, I assume this is your attorney." Mr. Chris asked.

"Yes I am. I'm Todd Ransom with Kirkland and Ellis." Stephanie turned her head quickly and looked at him. She couldn't believe Jason would call someone from Desmond's firm to represent her.

Todd looked at Stephanie and rested his hand on top of hers. He knew what she was thinking.

"What are the charges against my client?"

"Embezzlement!" The head of HR said.

"What proof do you have?"

The head of HR rep showed Todd a list of five accounts that had the missing funds.

"Is this all you have? Where is the evidence that points to my client?"

"These accounts belong to her, and besides, we heard she was going through a divorce and may not be able to afford some of the luxuries she's accustomed to."

"First of all, me going through a divorce has nothing to do with my finances. Do you not know how much you pay me? And another thing, I don't live beyond my means, my husband did, so that's how I acquired nice things. Since my husband has been employed at Kirkland and Ellis as an attorney, every paycheck that you have paid me for the last year, I have banked, so money is not a concern for me. Now let's get that straight!"

"Who else has access to these accounts?"

63

"Her CSP, our managers, and operations team."
And you just decided that she's the culprit? You can file these bogus charges against her if you want, but you better make damn sure you have evidence to support your claim, if not, she definitely won't have to worry about money when I'm through."
Another HR rep nodded his head to the officers and they left.

"We're still investigating, and when we are finished, we will be in contact."
Todd and Stephanie walked out of the conference room.

"Thank you so much for showing up. When I didn't hear from you or Jason, I just assumed you didn't want to take the case."

"No, not at all. Jason felt that if you knew ahead of time that I worked for Kirkland and Ellis, you wouldn't have hired me."

"And he was right." Stephanie said as she smiled up at him.

"They don't have a solid case against you. I think you were the easiest person to pin it on."

"I can't believe them. I worked my ass for this company for years."

CHAPTER 12

Stephanie was sitting in the kitchen eating lunch when her doorbell rang.

"Who could this be?" She said as she made her way to the front door.

When she opened the door, she was very surprised.

"What do you want? You got some nerve showing your ugly ass face here."

With a smirk on her face, Candice said nothing. She pulled the envelope out of her purse and handed it to Stephanie. Stephanie recognized the folder from her divorce attorney's office and snatched it out of her hand.

"And by the way, Desmond doesn't think I'm so ugly." She turned to walk away.

"Make sure this is the last time you ever step foot on my property, bitch!" Stephanie yelled and slammed the door.

Stephanie was furious. She tossed the folder onto the couch as she screamed.

"That fuckin bitch!"

Stephanie picked up her cell phone and dialed Desmond.

"How dare you send your little ugly bitch over here with the divorce papers! You fuckin coward! You got her doing your dirty work now!"

"What are you talking about? I haven't even signed the papers yet!"

Stephanie walked over to the couch, pulled the papers out, and examined the signature.

"I have the signed papers in my hand."

"What!"

Stephanie looked closely at the signature.

"Yep, she signed the papers for you."

"She what!"

65

"Yes, you heard me; she signed for you. I wonder what else she has signed for you, but that's not my problem, that's yours."

Stephanie disconnected the call and let the waterfall fall.

Susan walked over to Frank's desk. "Hey, have you heard anything from her?"

"No, I haven't. I will stop by her place on my way home."

"Okay, call me and let me know what's going on."

As Susan turned to walk away, an older and a younger female approached Susan at Frank's desk.

"Hello, I was told you are my daughter's boss."

"Are you Judy's mom?"

"Yes, I am."

"Have you heard from her? We have called, but we're not getting an answer?"

"No, we haven't. We are worried that something has happened. She was supposed to come to her sister's yesterday, and she never showed up."

"Did you check with the manager of the apartment complex?"

"No, we went to her apartment, but she didn't answer. I am going to see the manager when I leave here."

"Okay, let us know what you find out. This is not like Judy." Susan said as she walked them to the elevator, trying to pretend to be concerned.

Roger and Olivia were sitting in their den watching the news.

"Have you spoken with Desmond?" His wife asked.

"No, I haven't."

Olivia pulled out her phone.

"Who are you calling?"

"Stephanie."

Mouthing the words "Hang up" while swiping his hand at his throat in the cut motion.

"Hey Stephanie, I know it has been a while, but we need to catch up. Call me when you can, no rush."
Olivia disconnected the call and looked over at her husband who stared at her.

"What?"

"How would you feel if things were bad between us, and she called you to be nosey?"

"I wasn't just calling to be nosey. I wanted to check on her as well, but I guess you're right."

"Give her some time," Roger said.

Jason was sitting at home watching the game when he looked down at his phone. Someone sent him a picture of him and Stephanie at Friday's event with a message.

Your best friend's, wife? How low down are you?
Jason texted back.
Who is this?
Someone that's been watching you and Stephanie.

Jason looked around the room before calling Stephanie.
Stephanie sat on the couch as her phone rang. She picked her phone up to see who was calling. She didn't want to talk to anyone, not even Jason.

"Come on, Steph, pick up!"
It continued to ring and then went to voicemail.

"Stephanie, please call me ASAP! It's very important."

Later that evening, Desmond walked through the door. Candice looked up and quickly ended her call. She walked over to greet Desmond.

"Hey babe, how was work?"
He took his jacket off, set his briefcase down, and

unfastened his tie.

"It was okay. What did you do today?"

She reached up and to kiss him on the lips.

"Not too much of anything. Why do you ask?"

"I received a call from Stephanie this afternoon. She said you dropped off the divorce papers to her."

"Well, yeah, I saw them on Saturday when I was unpacking and I didn't want them to get misplaced, so I signed your name and dropped them off to her to speed up the divorce process. I hope that wasn't a problem?"

"A problem! You forged my name on those documents, so our divorce won't even be legal if she brings that up in court. Did you think my **WIFE** wouldn't know my signature! Desmond tried to remain calm, but he was pissed. And don't you know forgery is a crime? Is this something you have done before?"

"No, I haven't done this before, but I thought you wanted a divorce from your **WIFE!**"

"When it comes to my wife, I will handle things. I don't need you involved, do I make myself clear?"

"Sorry!"

Stephanie continued to sit when she heard a knock at the door. She ignored the knock. The front door opened. Stephanie looked up as her sister walked in.

Stephanie rolled her eyes, "I forgot you had a key."

"Awe Stephanie, I am so sorry to hear about you and Desmond. Why didn't you call me?"

Stephanie paused, trying to keep herself from crying again.

"I didn't want to bother you with my troubles. Not like you care anyway," Stephanie said under her breath."

"Girl, I'm your sister. That's what I am here for."

Her sister moved to hug her. The tears fell uncontrollably.

"Come on, let it all out. Sis, I thought you guys were happy."

Stephanie sat up. "So did I. Although I noticed he started working later and later. I would have never guessed it was another woman. I was so sure I was doing everything I needed to do as a wife."

"Are you sure?"

Stephanie eyed her sister.

"Yes!"

"I'm sorry. I didn't mean anything by it. Stephanie, now you know it doesn't matter how good of a wife you are, if they have that in their system to cheat, it is bound to happen."

CHAPTER 13

T**he** next day, Stephanie was in her office when her phone rang. She checked the caller id before answering.

"Hey Jason, what's up?"

"I know you're probably mad at me for not telling you about Todd, but I figured if you knew he worked with Desmond, you would not want him to represent you. I apologize, but I felt he was the right person to handle your case."

"I'm not mad anymore, and Jason thanks for contacting him."

"Can you join me for lunch today? There's something I need to talk with you about."

Stephanie hesitated, "Where Jason?"

"Where is your favorite restaurant?"

"I have several favorites, but I haven't been to Stacked Pickle in a while."

"Okay, well, let's meet there around 1. Is that okay?"

"Yes, I'll see you there."

Susan walked over to Frank's desk, "Hey, I just got a call from Judy's mom. The manager of her apartment complex let them in her apartment yesterday. She wasn't there. Her bed was made, and nothing seemed to be out of place.

"Frank, does she have a boyfriend?"

"No, she's not seeing anyone. What the hell is going on? Well, it looks like Karen was the last one to see her."

"What do you mean?"

"Judy worked late on Monday, and so did Karen."

"Really!"

As Stephanie approached Stacked Pickle, she bumped into Desmond's parents'.

She greeted them with a hug, but was cut off by her mother-in-law.

"Hi," Stephanie said.

Shrugging off Stephanie's hug, Mrs. Taylor said, "I think I've lost my appetite. Come on Des."

"Oh, so it's like that now. It doesn't matter what my side of the story is. " Stephanie said loud enough for them to hear.

"I can't believe it." Mr. Taylor said.

"Des." Mrs. Taylor called his name over her shoulder.

"I'm right behind you?"

Stephanie walked inside to find Jason already seated. He looked up and stood to greet her.

"Hey, how are you?"

He greeted her with a kiss on the cheek.

"I'm good, and you? You will not believe who I just ran into, and they had the nerve to not want to speak or even come in here once they saw me?"

"Who?"

"Desmond's parents."

"They were coming in here?"

"Yes, and when they saw me, they had a loss of appetite. And you won't believe this either. Yesterday, Candice stopped by and delivered the divorce papers. She forged Desmond's signature."

"No way!"

"Yes!"

"Did you tell Desmond?"

"I sure did. He had no idea what I was talking about. He said he hadn't even signed the papers. I looked at the signature, and true enough, it was not his signature.

"She is eager to get this divorce over. Well, you won't believe this either."

Jason pulled his phone out and showed Stephanie the text messages.

"Who is this?"

Jason shook his head.

"I have no idea, but whoever it is, they are watching us."

"This is all I need. I need to get away for a while."

Jason looked at her with a smirk on his face. Stephanie looked at him.

"What?"

"Well, you know I won that weekend getaway to the cabins. I could use a short vacation if you want to go?"

"Jason, I can't go away with you. How would that look?"

"What do you mean? We are friends, aren't we? We would have separate rooms."

Stephanie started thinking.

"Separate rooms! You know what, fuck it! I'm grown, you're grown."

"So are we going?"

"Yes, because God knows I need to get away right now."

Jason smiled.

"Ok! I'll get everything set up and send you the details later."

Five minutes later, their meal arrived. "Um, this looks so good."

Jason picked up his glass.

"Let's toast to new beginnings."

Stephanie picked up her glass.

Desmond sat at his desk with his fingers interlocked, looking out his office window. He turned around and pushed the button on the phone. He put it on speaker.

"Cynthia."

"Yes, Mr. Taylor.

"Get me Marcus Slay on the phone."

The phone rang three times before Marcus answered.

"Hey Marcus, it's Desmond."
"Desmond, how's everything, and how is Stephanie?"
"We are getting divorced."
Slight pause.
"Sorry, I didn't know. What can I do for you?"
"I need a favor completely off the books."

Stephanie was sitting on the couch holding a glass of wine, looking through a magazine when her phone buzzed. She picked up the phone off the table and read the message.

Stephanie- here are the details of where we'll be staying and the check-in time. As you can see, I gave you the room that has the massaging hot tub. With all you have on your plate, I think you will need this.

Stephanie smiled.
You couldn't be more right, but you won this trip. I'll be ok with whatever room I have. I just need a couple of bottles of Stella Rose Black, and I'm set.

I think we can make that happen.

Jason, you have done enough.

Stephanie, I'll pick you up at 9 am on Friday.

CHAPTER 14

Desmond was looking through some files when his phone rang. Desmond pushed the speaker button.

"Yes!"

"Mr. Slay is on line one," Cynthia said.

Desmond pushed the button on the phone.

"Yeah, what you got?"

"I haven't seen anything that raises any red flags yet, but if you want me to go underground then..."

"Do what you gotta do. I'll forward the money to your account later this afternoon."

Desmond pressed the speaker button to disconnect the call.

Desmond pressed the speaker button again.

"Cynthia."

"Yes, Mr. Taylor."

"Hold all my calls, I'll be out of the office for the rest of the day."

Michael got off the elevator and was headed for the hidden room in the basement. He moved the bookcase to the side that hid the door. He unlocked the door, opened it, and stepped inside. He removed the tape from Judy's mouth.

"I brought you some breakfast."

"I have to use the restroom first."

Michael untied her hands and feet.

"If you make any noise or try to escape, I will kill you. Do you understand?"

"Yes."

Still blindfolded, Michael escorted her to the bathroom and closed the door.

Inside the room, Judy removed the blindfold quickly. She scanned the room for an exit, but she didn't see one.

"Hurry up in there!"

"Don't rush me!" Judy yelled as she sat on the toilet.
Minutes later, Judy opened the bathroom door.

"Why are you doing this to me?" She said as she stood in the doorway.

"This is what happens to people who mettle in business that doesn't involve them."
Judy had just finished eating when they heard voices right outside the door.

"Don't make a sound."
Michael pointed the barrel of the gun to the side of her head.

"What's behind this door? I've never seen this door here before," Tom asked.

"Me either," Fred said.
Tom turned the knob, but it was locked.

"There has to be a key around here somewhere. Let's check with Joe," Tom said.

Todd agreed to meet with Stephanie at Starbucks instead of his office.

"Thank you for being so understanding about me not wanting to meet with you at your office."

"Oh, I understand," Todd said as he smiled.

"So what have you heard?"
Todd handed her the document. Stephanie read it and looked up at him.

"Are you serious? They're moving ahead with the charges? How ridiculous! What evidence do they have besides, they are my clients?"

"I don't know unless they have some evidence that they are holding onto until your court date."

"I don't see how. I did nothing wrong!"

"Calm down, I'm on your side. I will prove you did nothing wrong. They have to have evidence that you authorized the transfers; they have to tell us what accounts

75

the funds were transferred to, and they have to tie you to the funds and if they can't do that, I will ask that your case be thrown out."

"I want to counter-sue them."

"I have already filed a countersuit against them."

"Perfect!"

That night, Stephanie lay in the bed, clinching the covers between her legs.

"Hmm-hmm yes, oh yes, right there! Oh yes, I'm about to, ohhhhh!" She moaned.

A head came from under the covers as Jason climbed on top of Stephanie and penetrated her. Jason moaned.

Jason and Stephanie were making passionate love. Stephanie couldn't control the climax. She screamed as her body let go.

"Ohhhh!" Stephanie yelled.

Stephanie opened her eyes and sat straight up in the empty bed, and looked around. "Damn! Some dream," She said.

Friday morning, Jason stepped outside his home. He walked to his car and saw his tires were flat, and that someone had keyed the side of his car.

"What the fuck! Somebody done lost their damn mind!"

He walked around to the other side of the car to see if there was damage on that side. Both were flat.

"Damn!"

The white Nissan Rogue sat across the street as the driver inside watched as Jason checked out his car, but he never noticed it.

Jason quickly called Stephanie to let her know he will be a little late picking her up.

Two hours later, there was a knock at the door. Stephanie

went to open the door. Jason held two cups of coffee as his teeth clenched a bag of cheese Danish. Jason walked to the kitchen and sat the items down on the island.

"Good morning! How did you sleep?" Jason asked.
Stephanie smiled, "Better than I imagined."
Jason saw the luggage in the living room.

"Do you think you have enough luggage?"

"Look, a woman has to be prepared. You never know what the mood calls for."
Jason raised his hands in surrender.

"Ok, I know not to argue with a woman. I'm going to put these in the car."
As they stepped outside, Stephanie noticed Jason's car, "Oh my God! What happened to your car?"

"That's why I was late."
Jason put the luggage in the trunk.

"Someone flattened all four of my tires and keyed my car."

"Damn, who did you make mad?"

"I have no idea."

CHAPTER 15

Michael eased out of the room quietly. He made his way to the elevator without anyone seeing him. As he stepped onto the elevator, he heard voices coming.
Fred, Tom, and Joe walked past the elevator.

"What the fuck! Where did this door come from?" Tom asked Joe.
Fred looked around and ran his hand through his hair.

"Are we losing it?" Fred asked.
"Naw, I'm not crazy. I know this door was not here before," Tom said.

"Man, have you two been smoking? How can a door just appear out of nowhere? I'm outta here, I have worked to do."
Joe headed in the other direction as he shook his head.

Desmond's office

"Good afternoon, Handsome!" Candice said as she greeted Desmond.

"What are you doing here? I am busy. I have a lot of work to catch up on."
Candice and Desmond embraced. Candice melted into his arms and took in his smell.

"I know your busy, but I just had to come to see you."

"Can't it wait? You know we have dinner plans tonight. You are still going, right? I know you've been having some morning sickness because of the baby and all, but..."
Desmond helped her sit down on the sofa. He gave her a bottle of water from his office fridge.
Candice interrupted Desmond before he could finish his sentence.

"Yes, I'm fine! I will be ready for dinner."
Desmond sat at his desk and continued working. Candice

stared at him. She watched him focus on his task. She realized how smart and how handsome he was. Candice quickly snapped out of her thoughts. She reminded herself to focus on what she was there for. Candice walked over and stood behind him as he worked. She put her hands on his shoulders and began to massage them.

"Des? You remember my cousin Trina, right?"

"Yes."

He answered inattentively.

"I remember her."

"I was talking to her the other night, and she was telling me about her boyfriend. Rodney... something, I can't remember his last name. Anyway, she told me he got locked up on some BS murder charge and he needs an attorney."

Desmond looked up from his work and stared at Candice.

"O...kay."

"Des, let me finish. I was telling her that there are so many good attorneys here. I told her if she needed one, I could have you recommend one and she agreed."

"Oh, well that won't be a problem. Just give me a few days, I have to finish gathering the information for the two deposition hearings this week."

"I knew it wouldn't be, but that's not it entirely."

"What else does she want, a Pro-bono?"

Desmond was agitated and was shaking his head as he thought to himself about how this privileged white woman was asking for a favor for free.

"Look, tell your cousin that none of my colleagues do Pro-bono on murder cases unless they are high profile!"

"Desmond, calm down. No, she didn't ask for someone to take the case for free."

"Good! Because I damn sure wasn't about to ask anyone. Well, what else does she want?"

"She is more concerned about someone who will get her

man out of jail, especially because he is innocent."

"Aren't they all? And any of my colleagues can help her with that, I told you I just needed a few days."

"Well, actually," speaking seductively in his ear, "I was thinking about how smart and sexy you are, and how you're such a savage in the courtroom."

Candice knew her words would get Desmond excited. She pulled her underwear off and placed them on his desk. She was ready for him to take the bait. She knew that she was one step closer to setting her and Rodney's plan in motion. She loved how Desmond made love to her.

"Oh, so you think I'm a savage?"

"I know you are... especially in bed."

Candice leaned back against the desk. She placed Desmond's hand on her clit. She moved his finger up and down. Then Candice took two of his fingers and inserted them inside of her. She was eager for Desmond to release himself in her. She knew how much he wanted her right now from the bulge in his pants.

He walked over to his door and locked it. Staring at Candice, he picked up his desk phone.

"Cynthia, hold my calls for the next half hour, please."

He hanged up the phone, hurriedly walked around the desk, and lifted Candice onto his desk. He kissed her as he pulled her closer to him. He moaned in her ear as he raised her dress.

"I'm bout to unleash the beast!"

Candice smiled and closed her eyes. She let out a soft moan as he entered her forcefully.

"Unleash that beast, baby!" She whispered.

Down in the basement, the maintenance men were sitting at the table eating.

"Man, I know we ain't crazy," Fred said.

"I know, but Joe show in the hell thinks so," Tom said.

"I don't care what Joe thinks; I have been working here for over fifteen years, and I know every nook and cranny of this building," Fred said.

"I hear you man. What if something had been covering the door. That's the only explanation I can come up with," Tom said.

"Maybe there's a key in Joe's office somewhere."

Late afternoon, Michael was about to get in the car when his phone rang.

"Yeah! She cool! Nah, nobody saw me leaving. Oh shit, I forgot to move the shelf back over the door."

"Michael! Shit, let me run down and move it over the door."

Right before Karen left for the day, she took the elevator down to the basement. Karen exited the elevator. She looked around to make sure no one was around. Karen stopped at the door. She heard two men talking, so she ducked off into the stairwell.

"Let's try the door with this key here," Fred said.

"Dammit, it doesn't work. Let's just go and look for the key in Joe's office."

Joe called the men on the walkie-talkie.

"Hey, I need you guys at the loading dock."

"On the way, boss!

CHAPTER 16

Still in the stairwell, Karen called Michael back.

"We have a problem. We need to move her."

"Now?" Michael asked.

"Yes, now! They found the door. We don't have long before they get the door unlocked. Meet me in an hour." Karen disconnected the call.

Thirty minutes later, Joe was in his office going through his file cabinet looking for a file when he came across a small box. He opened the box to find some keys.

"Why would these keys be in here? Maybe one of these keys unlocks that door," He said aloud.

Joe made his way downstairs to the basement. He stood in front of the door. He tried several keys, but neither unlocked the door.

"Well, let's try this last one."

The door opened. Joe stood with his mouth hanging open.

Judy screamed underneath the tape that covered her mouth, "Help me!"

Joe removed the tape from her mouth.

"You gotta help me before he comes back."

Joe worked fast to untie Judy's hands and legs.

"Come on, let's get you outta here," Joe said.

Joe helped Judy to stand. They peeked their head out of the door before stepping out. Joe closed the door behind him and rushed her into his office.

Jason was standing at the reservation counter. He walked over to Stephanie holding the room keys.

"Here you go!"

They drove around the corner to their cabin, parked, and started unloading the car. When Stephanie opened the door, she was amazed.

Jason and Stephanie walked around the room admiring all the features.

"This is perfect!" Stephanie said as she smiled.

"And you have a lakeside view." Jason pointed to the window.

"This is what I need, Jason. I'm going to let my hair down and relax. No husband and his bitch to think about, no embezzlement, just peace and quiet."

"Well, I'll be at your beck and call. Whatever you need, let me know," Jason said.

"You have done enough. How can I ever repay you?"

"I'm just glad you came. I think we're going to have a great time."

Jason was so tall that he had to bend down to hug Stephanie. Stephanie smelled the cologne Jason had on. She looked up into Jason's eyes. Jason recognized the chemistry between them and pulled away. He wanted her, but he didn't want her like this.

Late that afternoon, Stephanie looked out the window at the lake when Jason walked up behind her.

"Ok, so I made dinner reservations for tonight. I'm going to let you get settled in, and I'll see you tonight."

"Ok," Stephanie said as she turned around to look at Jason. He grabbed his bags and walked into the connecting room. Stephanie stood there thinking.

She looked at her phone and saw her missed call from Olivia and began to listen to her message.

"Oh wow, I meant to call her back."

She sighed, took a deep breath, and sat down.

"It's been quite a while. This is going to be awkward."

"So, you have no idea who tied you up? Joe asked.
"No!"

"Okay, I'm calling the police."

"Wait, we have to be careful because we don't know

who's all involved," Judy said.

"Don't worry, I have a friend on the force. I'll have him come alone."

"I don't think it's a good idea that he comes here. What if the people behind my kidnapping are still here and sees him? What if they follow me home? I can't go back home until they catch this person."

Hearing Desmond as he pulled up, Candice sat on the couch and dialed the bridal shop. She wanted to make sure he heard her conversation.

"Hello, thank you for calling Vivian's Bridal. How may I help you?" The sales clerk asked.
Desmond walked in and heard Candice on the phone as he put down his briefcase, keys, and entered the living room.

"Hello, I want to schedule a fitting. There won't be a large bridal party so I can come much sooner, so do you have anything this week?'

"Yes, Tuesday at 2 pm."

"I'll take it!"
Desmond settled in as he listened to Candice give her contact info.

"Hey, I didn't hear you come in." Candice got up, headed over to the chair Desmond was sitting in, and sat on his lap and kissed him.

"I didn't want to interrupt you, so I tried to be courteous and quiet while you were on the phone."

"Thank you."

"So what are you getting fitted for?"

"My wedding dress."

"Wedding dress. Really!"

"Yes, I just want to be ready when you tell me your divorce is final!" Candice began to sob. "I don't want to have a baby out of wedlock and people calling him or her a bastard child all because."

84

He kissed Candice on her eyelids. "Shh, don't cry. My child will never be born out of wedlock, but let's take one thing at a time, okay?"

Michael and Karen unlocked the door and walked inside.

"Where the fuck is she?" Michael yelled as he looked around.

"And how am I supposed to know? You're the one with the key?"

"We're fucked!"

"Calm down. Did she see your face?"

"No."

"Then we are good. No one can tie us to the kidnapping." Karen tried to convince Michael.

Michael paced back and forth thinking. "Do you know where she lives?"

"Not off-hand, but I can get her information. Why?"

"Because we need to finish what we started. What if Judy shows up at work on Monday and tells everyone about what she saw on Susan's laptop? What if she tells them you were the last person to see her? They might put two and two together."

"Oh, I never thought about that."

CHAPTER 17

Desmond and Candice waited for their dinner.

"Baby, you look so good right now. It must be that pregnancy glow people talk about."

She smiled and pretended to blush. She was excited after the show she performed in Desmond's office earlier. She knew she was a step closer to becoming his wife. She knew she couldn't wait too much longer because Rodney reminded her every time she visited him that time was wasting.

"Thank you babe. I owe it all to you. I'm so happy that we are becoming a family. You, me, and our bundle of joy!"

"You are welcome. Thank you for being here for me."

"I wouldn't want to be anywhere else."

"I'm glad. You have shown me so much love and support."

"That's what a good woman does, Des, I will always have your back."

"You have had my back, and not only that, you know how to make me feel like a man."

"Aw, babe! That makes me happy to hear you say that. You work so damn hard every day. I feel like it's my job to make you feel good."

Desmond looked at his groin and smiled.

"Oh, I feel it. Especially when you do your magic with that tongue of yours!"

Desmond was teasing, but he was also serious. Stephanie could never satisfy him orally like Candice. Hell, Stephanie couldn't care less about even trying it.

Candice looked at Desmond in disbelief. She couldn't believe he said that even though it was true. She threw her napkin at him jokingly.

"Well, I do what I can, especially when I'm good at it! Besides, if I don't, what's going to make you come home at night."

"I come home because you are there."

"Well, I know your wife might still try to hold on to you. I don't want to lose you. Me and our baby," she looked down at her stomach, "Need you, Des."

"Candice, you have nothing to worry about. I don't want Stephanie."

He didn't believe his own words, but he hid it well.

"She has probably moved on anyway. I want to focus on you and our family."

Desmond couldn't believe he was saying the words he was hearing. He never thought he would be a father.

"I'm so happy you feel that way. I never thought I would be so happy with someone, especially someone so smart and handsome. I can't wait to spend the rest of my life with you, Desmond."

Desmond's stomach sank. He couldn't believe how fast things had changed. He wasn't even divorced yet, and now he is soon to be a father.

"Wow Candice, I never knew you felt that way. I know we started this thing as a fling, but we have come this far so fast."

Desmond's thoughts were racing. Should he marry Candice and make this child legit? Is this the right time? How will Stephanie feel about this? It was all too much at this moment. Desmond calmed his thoughts.

"Listen, don't go worrying yourself about the future. You don't want to stress. I heard it is not good for the baby. Besides, we should be celebrating. We're having a baby!'

"I agree! We should be celebrating."

Candice felt a quick tinge of remorse for carrying on this charade, but it quickly disappeared.

"Let's toast! To new beginnings!"

"To new beginnings!" Desmond said.

Desmond and Candice both took a sip of wine. They stared at each other with hidden thoughts.

Stephanie was still relaxing in the bed from a long nap when she heard a knock at the door.

"Come in."

Jason stuck his head inside.

"Are you okay?"

"Yes, I'm good. I slept longer than I had expected."

"I know I made dinner reservations for us, but if you would rather order in, that's fine with me?"

"You know, that sounds fantastic. We can have some wine and sit in the Jacuzzi afterward."

"That's what I'm talking about?" Jason moved further inside the bedroom.

"What do you have a taste for?"

"You know the Steak place we passed right before we turned into the resort smelled damn good."

"Okay, I will place an order and see if they will deliver. If not, I will go and pick it up."

"Sounds like a plan," Stephanie said as she lay across the bed.

After dinner, Jason and Stephanie sat in the Jacuzzi sipping on wine.

"You know I can't help but think about my situation. How am I going to clear my name? What if I go to prison for something I didn't do?"

Jason moved to sit next to Stephanie.

"Hey, let's not think like that."

He sat his wine glass down and turned her face to face him with his finger.

"I know you wouldn't do anything like that. You had no reason to and knowing how good Todd is, he will clear your name, trust me."

"I hope you're right, Jason."

"So, let's not think about your issues right now. I want you to enjoy this little getaway."

Just then, Paul Taylor's A Long Way Home played in the background.

"I love that song. I never knew you liked jazz, Jason."

"Woman, I thought you knew. Years ago, Desmond and I used to visit the Jazz Kitchen every week to hear some live jazz."

Jason and Stephanie's eyes locked. Stephanie turned away quickly. Jason eyed Stephanie up and down and felt a tingle in his manhood, so he turned his head.

Stephanie moved to the other end of the Jacuzzi. She took a sip as she eyed Jason with a smirk on her face.

"What's that look for?"

"No reason."

"Are you sure? Seem like something is on your mind."

Stephanie smiled.

"Maybe, maybe not."

Jason licked his lips, and it affected Stephanie.

Damn, this man is so fine. Stephanie thought to herself.

Jason looked at her and smiled. I wonder how she feels. If I'm lucky, maybe one day I will find out. He said to himself.

89

CHAPTER 18

Judy, Joe, and his wife sat at the kitchen table as his friend from the police force interrogated Judy.

"How many times do I have to tell you, I didn't see his face? I recognized his voice, but I can't put a face to the voice?"

"I'm sorry, but I am just trying to sort this out." Officer Knowland said.

"I know, but you're making me feel like I'm the criminal, not the victim."

"Is there someone you can stay with until we catch this person? It has to be a place where no one would think to look for you there." Officer Knowland asked.

"No, can I check into a hotel?"

"Sure!" Officer Knowland said.

"Oh no, she can stay here." Joe's wife said.

"Are you sure? I don't want to put you guys in any danger."

"Nonsense."

"But what about my car in the parking garage?" She glared at the officer."

"I'm afraid it has to stay. Whoever is behind this could be watching and waiting for you to show up and retrieve your car."

Michael sat in his car as he watched and waited for any sign of Judy. He looked at his watch and realized he had already been there two hours with no sign of her. He looked around to make sure he was not being watched. He was parked in a ducked-off area of the parking garage.

"Damn! I can't believe this bitch left her car here and didn't come back for it. Where can she be?"

Michael was tapping his fingers rapidly on the steering wheel.

"Come on! Come on! Where are you, lady! Come and get your car."

Michael's phone rang. He picked it up when he saw it was Karen calling.

"Yeah?"

"Hey, any luck spotting her?"

"Hell no! I have been here for two hours and nothing. Where the fuck can she be?"

"I don't know, but I hope she shows up."

"I don't think she is going to show up, and besides, it's late. We gonna continue this tomorrow."

"We? I'm not trying to be seen with you, that's why I came home, and you stayed. I do work with her, remember?"

"What the fuck you mean you not waiting with me? You got me involved in the kidnapping, so this is your mess too. You better disguise yourself, cause you gonna wait in this car with me."

"Michael, calm down. I know you don't like sitting and waiting, but you know why I got you involved. We did you a favor with the transfers, and so you returned the favor with the kidnapping. We both know what's at stake if we don't find that nosey bitch."

Michael was agitated, "Yeah, but now this shit has gone left, and I ain't going to prison for kidnapping!"

"Michael. Nobody is going to jail. We are going to find her. I have the information for her address and her mom's address, just like I told you I would."

"Good! But if we don't find her, she could tell what she saw. Then we both go down. I can't go to..."

Karen cuts Michael off.

"When you put this plan in motion, getting caught was not an option, and it still isn't. Trust me, you are going to find her, and besides,"Karen said flirtatiously, "There are plenty of incentives for you to get it done!"

Michael smiled. "Oh, yeah! And just what incentives you have in mind?"

"For starters, there's the money."

"I ain't thinking about money right now, quit playing."

Karen said teasing, "You'll find out as soon as you finish your parking garage assignment."

"Oh, I'm finished here. I'm coming to get my incentives, and I know it's wrapped in lace panties and a bra."

"Oh, you know me so well," Karen said seductively.

"Damn right I do. Put on those red bottoms too!"

Desmond entered the room. Candice quickly puts her magazine face down on her nightstand and picked up the remote.

"What do you want to watch or do you want me to put something on from our music bedroom playlist?"

"Neither, I'm more interested in why you are so intrigued by that magazine. I've noticed you looking at it when you think I'm not looking."

Candice smiled. "It's nothing really.'

She laughed as she got the magazine.

"It's just a baby room decorating magazine."

Desmond looked so emotional like he could cry.

Candice thought, I got him now.

"Come here and show it to me."

Desmond pulled Candice into his arms on the bed, and they looked through the baby magazine together.

Candice felt some kind of way about Desmond, but Rodney's voice rang in her ear.

"Don't fall for this dude," Rodney told her.

Stephanie lay awake in bed. She couldn't get her mind off

the dream she had last night about Jason. She imagined the feel of his tongue on her clit as she rubbed her fingers up and down. Then slid them inside her while the other hand rubbed her nipple.

Stephanie yelled softly, "Oh, Jason!"

Jason walked past Stephanie's room on his way to the kitchen when he heard her moaning his name softly. He stood there smiling, and then he knocked at her door.

Jason giggled, "Stephanie, are you okay in there?"

Stephanie jumped, she was embarrassed, and she hesitated to answer.

"Yes, I'm good."

She pulled the covers over her head as if he could see her.

Saturday morning, Karen rolled over to face Michael. She saw that he was awake and was looking up at the ceiling.

"Good Morning handsome." She said as she rubbed his chest.

"What are you thinking about, that explosive love-making session last night?"

Michael looked at Karen, kissed her forehead, and greeted her.

Stephanie lay in bed as the aroma of bacon, sausage, and coffee drifted into her room. There was a light tap at her door.

"Stephanie, breakfast is ready," Jason said.

"Okay, I will be right out. Thanks."

Jason and Stephanie sat in silence eating.

Jason laughed. "Sounds like you had a good time last night."

Stephanie's face turned red from embarrassment.

"I'm sorry, I couldn't help it!" Jason burst out laughing.

Stephanie looked up at him with a not so funny smirk.

"If you needed something, you could have come to me."

Stephanie's mouth flew open. Her eyes never left his as her hand accidentally hit her glass of orange juice."

"Oh, shit!"

"I got it!" Jason said.

Stephanie stared at Jason as he cleaned up her mess.

Her heartbeat was rapid. She was nervous and wanted to run back into her room.

After Jason cleaned up the mess. He took his seat and finished his breakfast.

"I'm sorry for what I said. I was out of line."

"You're fine."

CHAPTER 19

Laying in bed looking through the baby magazine. A diaper genie, what do you know about that?

"Enough to know I don't want the room to smell like somebody cut the cheese."

Desmond and Candice laughed.

"I just didn't think you would be interested or even know about those little things in our baby's room."

"Well, I am, and that's how I intend on being throughout our baby's life, starting with your regular doctor appointments. I know an OB you can see."

"No offense sweetie, but I'd feel more comfortable picking someone on my own. Your recommendation is someone you and your wife went to, am I right?"

"Yeah, you are and I get it."

Candice said loudly, "I don't want any more encounters like when we rented this condo."

"Ok, ok, baby calm down." He said as he rubbed her stomach.

The next morning, Candice was in the kitchen when Desmond walked in.

"Hmm, it smells good. What inspired all this?"

Desmond walked behind Candice, kiss her cheek, and grabbed a piece of bacon.

"I just thought I would fix my man a hearty breakfast."

Desmond pushed his manhood up against Candice.

"Baby, when you put it on me like you do, I always have a big appetite."

"Well, sit down. I'll make your plate."

"Now, that's what I'm talking about."

Candice handed Desmond his plate.

"Babe, I'm sorry for getting so emotional last night. I think it's my hormones. They are all over the place."

"You don't have to apologize. I'm told it's normal when you're pregnant, that you go through different emotions. I think it's cute, babe. Besides, it gives me more excuses to spoil you."

Candice got teary-eyed.

"See, I'm doing it again."

"Come here!"

Candice walked over to Desmond, who was sitting at the opposite end of the table. Candice sat on Desmond's lap.

"Look, I'm here for you and our baby. We are going to be ok. I don't want you stressing over anything. Concentrate on being beautiful and carrying our baby to full term so he's healthy. I'll take care of everything else, ok."

"How you know he's a he? There could be a she in here."

"I don't care, he or she is a part of you and me, so they'll be special, regardless."

"That's why I love you! You're going to be a great father."

Candice bends down to give Desmond a passionate kiss. Just then, her phone rang. The caller ID showed restriction.

"Are you going to get that?"

"It's not important. Everything important to me is right here."

Stephanie checked her voice messages. She had a message from her sister. She called her sister Sophia back, but it went to voicemail.

"Hi, Sophie, I hope all is well when this message reaches you. I just wanted you to know I took some time for myself and went to Gatlinburg to get away for a few days. Well, anyway, when I get back, we will talk."

Desmond walked to the reservation counter.

96

"Never mind, I see them."

"There's my boy."

"Pop! Mom."

Desmond kissed his mother on the cheek.

"Hello sweetie, how have you been?" Mrs. Taylor.

"I'm doing well, mom. Things are picking up at the firm. Plenty of cases to settle, so never a dull moment at Kirkland and Ellis."

"Well son, there's nothing you can't handle when you put your mind to it."

"You got that right, Pop! I learned from the best."

"Yes you did son. Your father was a good Foreman, but now it's time for us to live out our better days, seeing the world as he promised me we would. Isn't that right honey?"

"Yes dear, that is right"

Des Sr. leaned over and kissed Mrs. Taylor.

Desmond smiled.

"You two need to get a room."

"Son, how do you think you and your sisters got here?" They continued to kiss each other.

"That's right! A little kissing, a little hugging, and a lot of," Mrs. Taylor said.

Desmond smiled. "Ok, I get the point, now can we order before I lose my appetite."

"Well son, maybe with your next wife you'll find the love me and your father have. Speaking of, we ran into that girl the other day." Mrs. Taylor told Desmond.

"Who, Stephanie?" Desmond asked.

"Yes, we were both walking into Stacked Pickles."

"That's one of her favorite restaurants."

"Well, I lost my appetite, so your father and I left."

"Mom, you can't be mad at Stephanie. She did nothing wrong."

Desmond's phone rang, he looked at the screen and got up from the table.

97

"Excuse me, I have to take this."

"I don't think you should say anything else about Stephanie, after all, she is still his wife, and whatever happens is between them," Des said.

"I have never liked her."

Des sarcastically said, "You don't say. You hide it so well."

Mrs. Taylor made a funny face and rolled her eyes. Desmond returned to the table.

"Is everything ok son? His father asked.

"Yeah Pop. It's this case I'm working on."

"Sounds serious."

"Nothing my boy can't handle," Des said to his wife.

"Mom, Pops, do you guys mind if I take a rain check on lunch? I hired this private investigator to find some dirt for one of my cases, and he has some information for me?"

"An attorney's job is never done even to have lunch with his old parents."

"Speak for yourself. I'm not old. I'm well seasoned." Mrs. Taylor said.

Desmond got up and kissed his mother on the cheek.

"Lunch is on me. Love you all."

"Don't forget about our anniversary party next month."

"I wouldn't miss it for the world," Desmond said as he walked away.

Desmond walked into the establishment to see Marcus sitting at the bar. He was drinking a glass of wine as he watched the game. Desmond walked up to the bar.

"Let me get what he is having and get him another one." Desmond sat down.

"How's it going?"

"It's going." Desmond said. "So what you got for me?"

Marcus handed Desmond a large yellow envelope. Desmond opened the envelope, and his face drew a blank.

CHAPTER 20

Jason and Stephanie were getting out of the Jacuzzi. Jason stepped out first and extended his hand to Stephanie.

"Please take my hand, madam."

"Thank you."

While holding her hand, he pulled her in close to his body. He made eye contact with Stephanie, who quickly looked away.

Stephanie moved her head from side to side in a stretching motion.

"That was so relaxing. I'm going to get back in there one more time before we leave," She said.

"Steph, if your neck is stiff, you should let my magic fingers work that kink out."

"Um, I don't..."

"Come on, it's just a massage, I'll grab some blankets and put them on the bench part of the table for padding, and you'll feel great! At least I know my hands will."

Stephanie laughed and rolled her eyes playfully as she lay down.

While rubbing her back, he looked down at her.

"Steph, let me know how I'm doing ok. It's okay by me if you moan and say my name while I'm massaging you."

"Haha! You are so sure of yourself."

Candice was sitting at the visitor's table, waiting for Rodney. Rodney entered the visitor's room. He wasn't smiling when he saw Candice.

"Hi baby! Candice said.

"I called you; you didn't answer," Rodney said. Candice could tell he was angry.

"I know baby. He was still at the house when you called, and I couldn't answer."

"So what's going on? Any progress? I'm not getting a good feeling about this."

"Look, everything is going as planned. You have to trust me."

"Trust you! You out there, I'm in here, and I know he got his hands all over you."

"Baby, we got to stick to the plan. So if that means making him believe he's the only one for me then."

"Then what?"

"Baby look, I'm just trying to speed up the process that's all. He told me he got this and to let him handle it. I don't want him to get suspicious by breathing down his neck."

"Do you think our plan is gonna work? Cus if he told you to back off, then maybe."

"No, it wasn't like that. He just doesn't want me stressing because of the baby and everything. He's just being protective, that's all."

"So what makes you think he gon take my case?"

"I convinced him that my cousin needed an attorney for her man and that she only wanted the best."

"And he believed that?"

"Hook, line, and sinker. He's got some case's to clear out of the way and then he can focus on your case."

"I just hate the thought that he's touching you. I miss the touch of a woman. I'm missing you baby!"

"Baby, I miss you too! When I'm with him. I'm only thinking about you. I hurry through the motions with him. You are the only man that knows how to please me and make me come. Rodney was aroused at what Candice said."

"Lick them sexy ass lips. That's my girl."

Desmond decided to show Candice how much he adored her. He had cooked an intimate dinner for the two of them. He had set the mood with candles and soft music. Candice

100

walked in and was amazed at what Desmond had prepared.

"What is all this?"

"Well, I thought since you have done so much and have been very patient with me with all these cases. I thought I would show you how much I appreciate you."

Desmond held two wine glasses as he walked over to Candice.

"Wow! I don't know what to say. This is so sweet."

"Sparkling apple juice for my beautiful fiancé."

Candice smiled, "Thank you!"

Desmond pulled out the chair for Candice to have a seat.

"So how was your day? I missed you," Desmond said.

Candice took a sip.

"I can tell. It was good. Nothing too exciting. You know women self-care stuff. The spa and lunch with my cousin Trina. Nothing important."

"So, how is she doing?"

"I guess as good as to be expected. Trina wanted me to ask you when you think you would be ready to take on her boyfriend's case? Remember I told you her boyfriend was charged for murder?"

Desmond took a sip of wine. "Yes, I remember and I'm on it. I had my assistant pull his file, so I'll go through it on Monday."

"Really! Oh baby you don't know how happy that makes me… I mean my cousin will be happy to know this." Candice was excited.

"Well tell your cousin not to get too excited yet. Murder is a big charge, and unless this guy has a solid alibi. The burden of proof will be on us to convince a jury he didn't do it."

"Baby, I have faith in you. You are one of the best at what you do."

"Now, I thought you said I was a savage." Desmond said flirting."

101

Candice got up from the table and walk over to Desmond.

"Oh yes! You're a savage in the courtroom and the bedroom."

Candice kissed Desmond passionately. She grabbed his hand and led him away from the table.

Stephanie was all packed. Jason walked in with his suitcase.

"Are you ready?"

Stephanie looked around the room to make sure she wasn't forgetting anything.

"Yep! Jason, I can't thank you enough for inviting me. I feel ten pounds lighter."

"I'm glad I was able to help."

"You did, trust me. Jason, you're a good friend. Desmond is lucky to have you."

"Look, I hope this doesn't sound sleazy, but I enjoyed you this weekend."

"Jason, you are an amazing man, and from the first time we met, we connected like Wi-Fi."

"Wi-Fi!"

Jason laughed. "That's too funny. I'm going to have to use that one."

On the ride home, Stephanie was daydreaming. She missed Jason speaking to her.

"Hellooooo to Steph, is anyone home?"

"I'm sorry, I got lost in the scenery."

"Looks like it was more than the scenery that captured you."

Stephanie laughed. "I was thinking about what a good time I had with you this weekend. You are going to make someone a lucky and very happy lady."

Stephanie's cell phone rang. She saw it was Judy and quickly answered.

"Hey Judy."

"Hi Stephanie.

"I've been anxiously waiting to hear from you." Stephanie said.

"I know. So you haven't heard from Frank since we last spoke?"

"No, I haven't."

"Well, I have a lot of unbelievable and shocking stuff to tell you. Can I come over?"

"Yes, I'll call you when I get home in a couple of hours.

"Ok."

"That was Judy, and she says she's coming over to tell me what she found out."

"Great, I hope it's solid information that will help Todd clear your name."

"Exactly, I hate that I have to go back to this."

Rubbing Stephanie's hand. "Steph, you're not alone."

CHAPTER 21

Michael and Karen lay in bed after their first round of lovemaking when Michael sat up in bed.

Michael nervously said, "Damn! How could I have been so stupid?"

"What, what's wrong?"

"The security cameras in the building. If they check the footage, we're done!"

Why didn't you think about this earlier?

"I don't know. I have got to get in there and erase the footage."

"How do you know they haven't already viewed it?"

"Because we are not in jail. We should go now."

"Go now! No, it would look too suspicious if we went now. If they were to check the sign-in sheet and see we were there after hours, that would put my job in jeopardy. Let's go first thing in the morning, and we will do like we always do. You will pretend to ride up with me, and when you're finished in the security room, we will ride down together, and we will make it seem like you're carrying out a box for me to the car."

Back at Stephanie's, Jason got out and helped her with her bags.

"Thank you so much for helping me."

"My pleasure."

Jason turned to leave, but turned back to Stephanie.

"Steph." Standing in the doorway.

"Yeah."

"If you're not too tired of seeing this face, I was wondering if I could bring dinner back. Maybe Judy can join us?"

"I'm never too tired to see the warm face of a friend. A

handsome friend at that."

"I'll take that. While you get comfy, I'm going to go change and bring dinner back."
Stephanie shut the door and leaned against it. She sighed and looked up.

"God, please let Judy have good news."
An hour later, Stephanie's doorbell rang.
Stephanie looked through the peephole and saw it was Jason. She opened the door,"Come right on in!"

"Yes, ma'am"

"Ooh, that smells good! What did you get?"
They unloaded the food.

"I got some BBQ from this neat little place out west called Hank's BBQ, and it is so good. Wait until you try their loaded potato with brisket."
Jason playfully pointed at Stephanie's stomach.

"Save room for dessert because I brought peach cobbler."

"I have plenty of room. I'm just anxious about what Judy found out."

"Will she be here soon?"

"I think so, but let's just bless the food and dig in."
They bowed their heads.

Judy was in the car with Mrs. Augustine. She was dropping her off at Stephanie's.

"Make a left at this next corner, and her house is the 4th or 5th one on the right-hand side. Thank you for giving me a ride. I don't have any cash. I don't have my purse or wallet after they kidnapped me.

"No problem, which house?"

"That one with the porch light on with the two cars in the driveway."

"Let me know when you're ready to come back."

"Okay, and this wig you got me wearing looks pretty good on me."

"Don't forget these."

She handed Judy a pair of sunglasses.

"Thanks."

"Doorbell rang."

Stephanie doesn't recognize the female at the door through the peephole.

"I wonder who this is?"

"It's not Judy?"

"Nope."

"Here, let me get the door."

Jason walked over to the door and opened it. Stephanie stood behind him.

"Hello, may I help you?"

"Yes, I'm here to see Stephanie."

Stephanie stepped from around Jason when she recognized the voice.

"Oh my God! I didn't recognize you. Come on in. Oh, and I like that Cher vibe you got going on."

"Thanks, but it's not by choice."

Judy said as she followed Stephanie into the kitchen.

Judy snatched the wig off and sat in a nearby chair.

" Do you want some water?"

"Yes, please."

Judy sat around the kitchen table. She told them her story.

"Joe and his wife offered me their place to stay as long as I needed it, but I don't know them that well, and I really don't want to impose."

"I got you into this mess, so it is only right that you stay with me. Besides, no one would expect you to be here, and I would love the company."

Judy looked over at Jason and back at Stephanie.

"Are you sure?"

"Of course. Todd isn't going to believe his ears

I can barely believe what I've heard.

"Neither can I. I don't even know what to say. How did either of us get mixed up in this?"

Well, after hearing all that, at least for tonight, would you feel better if I slept on the couch? Jason asked.

"Yes." Judy and Stephanie said yes in unison.

"May I use your phone. I need to thank Joe and his wife for their hospitality and let the detective know where I'll be staying?"

"Sure, and I'll get you a phone tomorrow. You need to have one for when I'm not home. Are you hungry? We have plenty."

"No, I already had dinner, but thanks anyway."

After returning from dropping Judy off Mrs. Augustine joined her husband on the couch. They were lying on the couch watching Law and Order about a murder in a downtown alley, and the outside security camera caught the murder on camera.

Joe looked at his wife. A light bulb had just gone off in his head.

"Man, we have security cameras all over the building, and I bet you anything, I will see who kidnapped Judy."

"Oh my God! I didn't even think about that. As much as I love to play detective, I can't believe I didn't think of that."

"As soon as I get to work in the morning, that will be the first thing on my to-do list."

The alarm went off at 5:00 am. This will give Michael just enough time for him to get in and out of the building before the workers arrived. Michael got dressed in record time.

At Joe's, it was 5:30 am, and Joe was dressed. His wife had just finished packing his lunch. He was eager to see the footage from the first day Judy went missing.

"Are you ready, babe?" Michael asked.

Karen walked into the living room with her purse and coat in hand.

Joe arrived at the parking garage in record time.

Michael and Karen got out of the car in the parking garage. They rode the elevator down to the lobby. Michael had to sign in at the security guard's desk.

Michael and Karen walked over to another set of elevators. Karen pushed the up button. Seconds later, the elevator doors open, and Karen and Michael hopped on and made sure they were the only ones in the elevator. Karen rode the elevator to her floor, and before the doors open, Karen said, "Remember to call me as soon as you finish, and I will get on the elevator and meet you with a box for you to take to your car."

"Bet," Michael said.

Karen hopped off the elevator, and Micheal pushed the button to the basement. He rode down and hoped and prayed no one was in the security room. He tried to time it when whoever was in the security room went on break.

The elevator doors opened to the basement. Michael peeked out to see if anyone was around and when he didn't see anyone, he got off the elevator.

Joe had just signed in at the security desk. He made his way over to the elevator for the basement.

Michael walked swiftly down the hall that led to the security room. The only sounds heard were the sound of his shoes on the concrete floor. The hall seemed longer than ever. It was almost spooky.

Michael approached the security room. He peeked through the window and saw Richard with his coat getting ready to go out for a smoke break.

"Perfect timing," He said.

In the security room, Michael pulled up the footage from the day of the kidnapping. It took him about three minutes

108

before he saw what he was looking for. He saw Judy in the basement. He saw himself as he brought food down to her. He played the footage forward, and he saw Tom and Fred as they tried to unlock the door, and then he fast-forwarded and saw Judy being escorted out of the room by Joe.

Joe stepped off the elevator and walked down the hall that led to the security room. Joe turned the corner and ran into Richard.

"Just coming back from break?" Joe asked.

"Yeah, I got to have that morning smoke with my coffee."

Michael was still in the security room when he heard voices coming. He was in the process of deleting the footage for that week.

"Come on Shit!" Michael said nervously.

Michael heard the door open, and in walked Richard and Joe. He slipped out through the side door. "Damn, that was too close."

"Hey, I need for you to pull up the footage from Monday," Joe said.

Richard sat down and pulled up the footage. He went back and forth. "That's weird. There's no footage for this week at all."

"Is it possible that someone deleted it?"

"Yes, but why would someone want to delete it?"

CHAPTER 22

Stephanie sat in the chair next to Todd, nervously waiting for the Preliminary hearing to begin. She closed her eyes, said a quick prayer, and blew out a slow-long sigh.
Todd looked at Stephanie. He picked up on her nervousness.

"Hey, you okay?"

"Yeah, I'm just ready to get this over with. I can't believe I'm sitting here going through this right now. This is some bullshit. I don't know who did this or why, but I shouldn't be here."

"It's okay Stephanie, calm down. That's why I'm here."

"Yeah, you're here, but you ain't in my seat. This is… I don't even know what to think anymore."
Todd looked at his watch and put his hand on Stephanie's shoulder.

"Just a few more minutes until the hearing starts, relax. I got this."

"Okay, I'll trust you this time."
Todd smiled, "It's like that! You tough, huh?"

"Damn right! My career and everything I have worked so hard for are on the line. Wouldn't you be if it were you?"

"I guess I would," Todd said.
The bailiff asked everyone to rise as the Judge entered the courtroom and took the bench.
The judge looked over the case notes. He made a note of the date and time and the case number, state, her name, and noted that this was the case of Charles Schwab versus Stephanie Taylor. The judge addressed the prosecuting attorney and Todd.

"Are we hearing this case today, Mr. Wright?" The judge asked.

110

"Yes, Your Honor." The prosecuting Attorney Wright said.

"Mr. Ransom?"

"Yes, Your Honor," Todd said.

He addressed both attorneys and focused his attention on them.

"Are there any preliminary motions that need to be dealt with before we proceed?"

"No, not from Charles Schwab, your Honor," Attorney Wright said.

"Yes, your honor. If you don't mind, I would like to meet in your chambers and not the bench," Todd said.

Stephanie looked at Todd with questioning eyes. The prosecutor also looked over at Todd.

Before the proceedings, Todd and the prosecuting attorney had been in talks about the hearing. Several issues came up, but Attorney Wright was not sure what Todd was up to.

"Okay, we will take a short recess to meet in my chambers and reconvene in just a moment."

Fifteen minutes later, the judge and the attorneys returned from the judge's chambers.

"In the matter of Charles Schwab versus Stephanie Taylor, it's Charles Schwab's burden. Mr. Wright, you may call your first witness." The judge said.

"Your Honor, we call to the stand Susan Smith."

"Ms. Smith, if you would please take the stand."

Susan walked toward the judge and stood behind the stand. The bailiff raised his right hand, and Susan did the same.

"Ms. Smith, do you swear to tell the truth, the whole truth and nothing but the truth so help you God?"

"I do."

"Ms. Smith, please state your name for the judge," Attorney Wright asked.

"My name is Susan Smith."

"Ms. Smith, who do you work for?" Attorney Wright asked.

"I am the Supervisor for Account Managers at Charles Schwab."

"Did you call HR on the morning of March 25, 2020, to report fraudulent activities on five different clients' accounts?"

"I did."

"Please describe in detail what happened that morning."

"I received a call from five different clients stating that unauthorized funds been transfered from their accounts. Each account had different amounts withdrawn. I gathered the information on the accounts and checked them myself to be sure that there were discrepancies. I saw who the account manager was on each of the accounts, and I immediately notified HR of the issue."

"Tell us what happened that afternoon, after HR was notified."

"Mr. Chris from HR came to my office, and we discussed what I discovered. I showed him all the information, and he then decided that the defendant, Mrs. Taylor, be suspended until further notice. Mr. Chris called Stephanie and asked if we could meet with her in her office. Mr. Chris and I walked to Mrs. Taylor's office and informed her about the missing money from the accounts she managed."

"Was Mrs. Taylor aware of why you called the meeting?"

"She was not told by Mr. Chris or myself the purpose of the meeting beforehand."

"Were there others in the meeting?"

"No, Mr. Chris decided that it would be best that it only be myself and him, and later two officers escorted Mrs. Taylor from the premises in case she became violent."

"What was her response to the news that there was

112

money missing from those accounts?"

"She asked if we thought she took the money or had something to do with the missing money. We explained to her that those accounts were managed by her alone and that no one else had access to the accounts."

"Did she deny withdrawing or transferring any of the funds in any of the five accounts?"

"She did. She explained that she had no reason to take the money. We explained to her that her user id had been used to approve the wires, so Mr. Chris decided that it would be best if she was suspended until further notice."

"Was there anyone there to assist with making sure Mrs. Taylor gathered her things and only her things as she left the premises?"

"Yes, two officers stood there and made sure she took only her belongings, and then they escorted her out of the building."

"I have no more questions for the witness, your honor." Attorney Wright said.

"The court will now stand adjourned until 1 pm this afternoon."

"Mr. Ransom, would you like to cross-examine the witness?"

"Yes I would Your honor."

Todd stood and walked over to stand in front of the witness.

"Susan, how long have you known Mrs. Taylor?"

"Oh, for about ten years. We're best friends."

"Okay, so you know her pretty well, wouldn't you say?"

"Yes, we're like sisters. Sometimes I know what she's thinking before she says it."

Susan chuckled.

"So, what type of person would you say Mrs. Taylor is?"

"She's a very loving and loyal person."

"So loyal that she would embezzle money from a company that she worked her butt off for?"

Todd looked over at Stephanie and then Mr. Wright.

"Isn't it true that you admire Stephanie?"

"Yes, I admire her. She helped me build confidence in myself. She helped me with my weight loss. She has always been there for me when I needed her."

"Like the time you fell behind on some of your bills, and she loaned you money that you have never paid her back for?"

"Well…," Susan said.

Mr. Wright stood. "I object your honor!"

"Is this leading to somewhere?"

Todd faced the judge.

"Yes, it is."

"Objection overruled."

Todd focused his attention back on Susan.

"Isn't it true that you and several other employees have access to those accounts?"

"Yes, we do."

"You said earlier that Mrs. Taylor was the only one that had access to those accounts. So which is it?"

"I mean… I didn't mean to say she was the only one with access."

"Your honor can we make note that Ms. Smith just lied under oath." Todd turned to look at the judge.

"Noted." The judge said.

"Isn't it true that you wanted to be Stephanie?

"Excuse me."

"You heard me. Isn't it true that you had an affair with Stephanie's husband? You were secretly jealous of Stephanie, so when you found an opportunity to destroy her, you took it!" Todd said as he raised his voice.

"No, no, that's not true."

114

Susan looked over at Mr. Wright as he stood again.

"I object, Your Honor. He is badgering the witness!"

"No more questions, Your Honor."

Todd walked back to his seat as he smiled.

Todd whispered, "With a friend like that, who needs enemies."

Stephanie whispered, "Now she looks like the one that framed me."

"That was my angle."

"Your Honor, my client would like a continuation." Attorney Wright said.

The judge looked at his schedule.

"We will reconvene three weeks from today at 1 pm."

CHAPTER 23

Susan sat in her office waiting for Karen's arrival. Karen walked past Susan's office smiling and greeting everyone. Susan stuck her head outside of her office. Karen, when you get settled can you come to my office?

"Sure, just give me a sec."

Karen shut the door behind her. She took a seat in front of Susan's desk.

Frank watched Karen walk inside of Susan's office. He could tell Susan was upset about something, so he walked over to the copier, right next to Susan's office.

Susan was angry, "What the fuck is wrong with you? Why would you send another transfer?"

"Michael wanted me to do one last transfer."

"And why would you listen to that idiot! Stephanie is no longer here, and she does not have access to these accounts anymore."

Frank stood at the copier pretending to be organizing his papers, and listening through the paper-thin walls.

"Oh my God! I didn't think about that. Do you want me to reverse it?"

"It's a little too late for that. The client has already spoken to Jessie about it, and he wants me to find out which computer it was sent from."

"What are we going to do?"

"Please tell me you didn't send it from your laptop?"

"No silly, I sent it from Judy's laptop. Oh, and I forgot to tell you, we have another problem." Karen leaned and whispered, "She's missing from the basement."

Susan threw up her hands.

"Damn! Can't you guys do anything right?"

"I guess we did something right because I didn't hear you complaining when you got your big payoff."

Karen rolled her eyes.

Michael sat in his car and watched as Joe pulled off. He waited until he turned the corner before getting out of his car. He never noticed the neighbor watching him from her living room window as he made his way to the front door. Micheal knocked twice before Joe's wife answered. Joe's wife opened the door to find a stranger there.

"Can I help you, sir?"

"Is Joe here?"

"I'm sorry, you just missed him."

Michael pushed his way inside the home and shut the door behind him.

Joe's wife screamed, "Who are you, and what do you want!"

"Where is she!"

"Where is who?"

Michael slapped her and she fell onto the couch.

"Don't play stupid with me you old bitch! You know who I'm talking about?"

Joe's wife reached for her cell phone, but Michael yanked it out of her hand.

"Now I am going to ask you one more time, where is Judy!"

"I don't know who you are talking about!"

Michael grabbed her up off the couch and guided her down the hall to the first bedroom.

Michael walked to the first bedroom and pushed Joe's wife down on the bed as he checked the closet and up under the bed. He yanked her up and headed for the second bedroom.

In the second bedroom, he made Joe's wife sit on the bed as he checked the closet and under the bed. He looked back at her, "You know it didn't have to be like this, but your husband stuck his nose where it didn't belong."

Michael approached Joe's wife on the bed. He grabbed

117

pillow and covered her face with it as he pushed her back on the bed. Mrs. Augustine fought to remove the pillow, but her strength did not match his. Micheal held the pillow over her face until she was no longer moving. Then he panicked. He rushed out and left the pillow over her face.
Later that afternoon, Joe walked through the door wondering why the front door was open.

"Honey, I'm home. Why was the front door open?" Joe yelled. Joe walked into the kitchen, but his wife wasn't there. He headed down the hall, and when he came to their bedroom, he stopped in his tracks. He found his wife in bed with a pillow over her face. Joe ran to her side and tossed the pillow to the floor. She was unresponsive, and then he noticed she was blue and her body was cold.

"No! No! Why, who would do this?"

Michael paced back and forth as he awaited Karen's arrival. Karen walked through the door.

"What was so important that I had to leave work early?"

"I killed her?"

"You killed who?"

"I went there looking for Judy, but she wouldn't tell me where she was, so I smothered her."

"You, what! Did anyone see you leave?"

"No."

"Are you sure?"

"I don't know. I was in and out. I didn't even think about anyone seeing me."

"You're going have to lay low, and also, that transfer you asked me to do, raised a red flag so we cannot make any more transfers."

"We have to."

"No, we're not!"

"I still owe 100k."

"Too damn bad. You better find another way to pay off your gambling debts."

"How much money do you have?" Michael asked.

"Don't worry about it. My money ain't your money, and besides, you got the same amount of money that we did. It's not my fault you wasted your money instead of paying off your debt."

"What! Where is this coming from?"

"I'm just tired of you trying to manipulate me."

"You been hanging around that black bitch I see. Letting her fill your head with shit. Don't let her get you an ass whipping."

Karen gave Michael an evil look, "Yeah, try it!"

Joe sat on the couch as he sobbed. The coroner left with his wife's body and the detectives talked to each other.

"None of the neighbors outside saw anything," One of the detectives said.

"Well, the CSI investigator guy is here now. I hope he finds something to go on," The second detective said.

The next morning, Ms. Sherry the neighbor who lived across the street from Joe, knocked on his door. Joe opened the door. Joe had not handled the murder of his wife well.

"Hi, Sherry! Today isn't a good time." Joe said full of emotions.

"I'm so sorry to bother you. I understand how hard this must be for you."

"No, I don't think you do. My wife was the nicest person I've ever known, she wouldn't hurt a fly. I just don't understand how someone could do this to her."

"Joe, I don't want to add any more on you than you can handle, but I have to tell you something."

"Well, come on in then. Let's go to the kitchen."

Joe was emotionally exhausted from the death of his wife.

He stood facing the stove with tears running down his face. Still facing the stove, he asked. "What is it you need to tell me?"

"The other morning, I saw a car parked in front of your house."

Joe turned around to Sherry.

"Did you see who was in the car?"

"Yes, I saw a man walk up the walkway. I didn't think much of it at first, but when I heard what had happened, I put two and two together."

"Sherry, this is great! This is the most information the detectives have so far."

"Just let me know what I can do to help."

"I need you to tell him what you saw."

"Absolutely!"

Joe got emotional again.

"Joe I'm so sorry! Sherry was a beautiful woman, and I'm truly going to miss her."

"Yes, I know. You two really hit it off. She spoke highly of you all the time. What I wouldn't give to have her back."

"She loved you very much. I remember her telling me how you two first met. We laughed so hard."

Joe tried to smile through the tears.

"I can't believe she told you that story, we said we wouldn't ever tell anyone that story."

"Oh Joe, she loved you so much. She wanted to tell the world how much."

"I guess you're right," Joe said.

"Let me get out of your hair. I only came over to tell you what I saw. Maybe this will help the police find out who did such a horrific thing to such a beautiful person."

"I can't thank you enough."

"There's no need to thank me, it's my civic duty. We have to protect our neighborhood. Just let me know if there is anything else, I can do to help."

120

Right after Sherry left, Joe called the detective.

"Yes, my neighbor Sherry came over and said she saw a man here yesterday."

"Where is she now?" Detective Morris asked.

"She's at home."

The detective took out his notepad.

"What's her name? Do you think she would mind if I came over to ask her a few questions?"

"Her name is Sherry Davis and she said she'd be happy to help, but I don't know if she wants the neighborhood to see the police showing up on her doorstep."

"If you don't think she wants us to come to her. Do you think she would come to the precinct as soon as possible and give a description while it's fresh in her memory?"

"Yeah, that shouldn't be a problem."

CHAPTER 24

That evening, Stephanie and Judy sat at the kitchen table having dinner when the doorbell rang.
Judy and Stephanie looked at each other.

"Oh my God! Who could it be," Judy said.

"Calm down, no need to worry, just go to the bedroom, and I will come and get you when the coast is clear."
Stephanie went to the door and opened it to find Frank standing there.

"Hey, what are you doing here?"

"I have got some news for you. Can I come in?" Frank said.

"Sure."
Stephanie stepped back and allowed Frank to enter.

"Have a seat. Can I get you something to drink?"

"Yes girl, I need a glass of wine. I can't believe what I heard this morning at the office. I have been replaying it in my mind all day. I had to be sure I heard everything correctly."
Stephanie returned with two glasses of wine and plopped next to Frank on the sofa.

"So what is so important that you had to come over here this time of the evening?"

"Well, this morning, I saw Karen walking into Susan's office. I could tell by Susan's face that she was upset about something."

"Hmph, ain't no telling those those two. They probably up to no good."

"Listen, so you know me, I had to find out what was going on, so I went to go stand at the copier."

"Of course!" In true Frank form.

"So what did you find out?"
Just then, Judy peeked her head around the corner trying to

get Stephanie's attention.

"Psst psst!" Judy said.

Frank looked up and screamed at the sight of Judy nearly spilling his wine.

"What in the hell? Judy, is that you?"

"Judy, I am so sorry! I forgot to come and get you."

Frank looked confused and surprised.

"Where? When did? How long have you been here?"

Judy opened her mouth to try to explain, but Frank cut Judy off.

"And You."

Frank looked at Stephanie in bewilderment.

"You had her here all this time?! What the hell is going on Stephanie?"

"Listen Frank, I will explain all of this later. Right now, I need you to tell me what you heard at the office this morning."

Frank hesitantly spoke as he observed Stephanie and Judy.

"Where was I? Y'all done got me all confused, hell."

"You were telling me about Susan being angry about something, and Karen walked into her office."

"Oh yeah! So, this heffa walks in, and Susan gives her the third degree about making another transfer."

Frank continued to tell them the story.

"Them dirty bitches. I need to call my attorney and let him know what is going on. Now if you want to fill Frank in on your situation, Judy you can do that."

Stephanie began to talk to herself as she walked into the kitchen to get her phone.

"These bitches got me fucked up. Oh, they tried it. I'll give em that. Stupid asses."

Judy and Frank sat at the kitchen table.

"So why have you been over here? And why haven't you been at work? Your mom and sister have been up to

123

the job looking for you! And why is your car is still in the parking garage. And why haven't you returned any of my calls. What the hell is going on"

Judy explained the situation.

"So you see, that's why the police wanted me hidden. Here's my number, but don't save my name, and be careful what you text me."

"Ok, I can't believe all this went down, and people are walking around as nothing has happened."

"Yeah, tell me about it."

"And on top of that still making transfers and blaming others."

"What are you talking about?"

Stephanie walked in.

"Yeah, what are you talking about?" Stephanie asked.

"I forgot to mention when I was ear hustling outside Susan's office. That heffa Karen said she used Judy's laptop for the last transfer. Can you believe that?"

"For real! I hope they throw her under the jail."

Stephanie picked up her phone and dial her attorney's number.

"Hey Todd, this is Stephanie. Please give me a call as soon as possible. I have some very important news that is going to blow this case wide open and prove my innocence."

Stephanie puts her phone down and smiled.

A few minutes later, Stephanie's phone rang. She saw that it was Todd and she excitedly picked up.

"Hello Todd, and thanks for calling me back so quickly. I have great news."

"So I heard on my voicemail. I can't wait to hear it, go ahead and tell me."

"I finally have proof that I did not take the money. I am innocent, just like I said."

"Well, I need to decide if it's proof, what information do

you have?"

"Well, Frank my co-worker just came over to tell me what he heard Susan and Karen discussing in the office this morning."

Stephanie began to tell Todd what Frank heard.

"I know, right!"

"Are you sure? I mean this is great news, but we must have concrete proof. Will he be willing to testify to this in court?"

"Yes! I don't see why not. He also said that Karen mentioned someone named Michael. I think it's her boyfriend Michael. The same Michael that I used to date."

"Wow... this is big news. It gives us more to investigate before the next court date."

"I know that is why I called you. I know you have to do some digging."

"Thanks for the information, Stephanie."

"No, thank you, Todd, for taking my case with all that I am going through with my husband. I know I was skeptical about anyone from that office, but you proved me wrong."

"You know, that is what a professional does. I get paid to help my clients regardless of their personal affiliations unless it harms a case.'

"Well, I'm glad I have you on my side. Now I can move forward with my life and work, thanks to you."

"You're very welcome. I'll talk to you soon."

CHAPTER 25

The next day, Joe and Sherry arrived at the precinct around noon.

"Sherry I'm so glad you came forward," Joe said.

"It's the right thing to do."

Ms. Sherry gave the sketch artist the description and he drew the perp and showed his sketch to her and Joe.

"Oh my God!" Ms. Sherry said as she jumped.

"Yes! That's him."

Joe looked at the sketch.

"This face looks very familiar to me. He looks like a guy that used to work with me."

The detective pulled Michael's mug shot up.

Joe pointed at Michael's picture.

"Why does he have a mug shot? What did he do?"

He was arrested for fraud four years ago." The detective said.

"Really! I would have never thought that about him." Joe said as he shook his head.

"This explains why his fingerprints were in your house." Joe clinched his jaw, and took a deep breath.

"So Michael killed my wife? But why?"

The detective walked in with a cup of water.

"Here you go!" The detective handed Joe the water and he ignored it.

Sherry grabbed the cup.

"Joe, drink some water!"

"I just can't believe this! Why would he kill my wife? I have never had any issues with him."

"Were there ever any issues at work? Do you know why he no longer works there?"

"Hell, everybody knew he was sleeping around with Karen."

The detective took out his notepad and began to write.

"Karen, who is Karen?"

"Just one of the staff on the top floor. She works for Charles Schwab."

"Why would that be a problem they're both consenting adults?"

"Because it was against company policy."

"How did the company know they were together?"

"I guess when you get caught having sex in the bathroom, it doesn't take long for it to get out, so they fired him."

"But not Karen?"

"She's in management, he's in maintenance. You do the math! What does this have to do with my wife's murder?"
I'm not sure yet. Look, we're going to get this guy. I'm going to look into these leads. I will be in touch. Thanks, Sherry your information was a big help."

Stephanie and Sophia sat at the table waiting for their server. Sophia looked at the menu.

"I see so many things I like. I see why you like to eat here."

"Yes, and I already know what I want, so take your time and look over the menu, or do all pregnant women just eat pickles and ice cream?"
They both laughed as the server approached.

"Hi, my name is CeCe I'll be your server. Would you like to start with a drink or water while you look over the menu?"

"We'll take water, thank you," Sophia said.

"Okay, I'll be right back."

"Uh, you gonna order my food too?"

"Sorry, but I can't wait to hear what made you decide to take a trip all of a sudden in the middle of all the chaos that has broken loose in your life lately?"

"Thanks a lot, sis. Chaos is that…"

"Sorry, I guess I'm having pregnancy brain because I couldn't think of a better phrase to categorize these multiple situations. I didn't mean anything by it."

"Okay well, Jason asked me to accompany him to the cabin," Stephanie told Sophia how helpful Jason had been and how she did him a favor and in return, he asked her to join him on the trip.

"Is this the real reason Desmond left you because you were sneaking around with his best friend?" Sophia said with a sarcastic tone.

"What! Did you not hear what Desmond did? I love Desmond and…"

Sophia cut her off. "And what, so you made up this story about him leaving you so you can conveniently have a rendezvous with Jason?"

Looking hurt and confused, Stephanie grabbed her purse and threw money on the table.

"You know what! I'm so sick and tired of trying to get along with you and you never having my back. The one time I thought you'd have some empathy, you managed to fuck that up too!" Stephanie stormed out.

CeCe saw the body language as she started to approach the table but decided to turn around.

Karen was on the phone when her assistant knocked and stuck her head in.

"There is a Detective Roy here to see you."

"Hey, let me give you a call right back."

Karen looked at the assistant nervously.

"Did he say what he wanted?"

"No!"

Karen fidgeted with papers on her desk.

"Ok, send him in!"

Detective Roy walked into the office.

"Hi, Karen!"

"Yes detective?"

"Roy, Roy Davidson, but Roy would be fine."

"Ok Roy! How may I help you?"

"I'm looking for Michael. Do you know where I could find him?"

"Um... Michael, no why would you think I would know where Michael is, he doesn't work in the building anymore."

"Yes, I've been told."

"So why would you come here looking for him?"

"I was told that you two are dating, which is why I came here."

"Were!"

"Excuse me!"

"Were dating! I haven't seen Michael in months."

"Where exactly was the last time you saw him?"

"He asked me out for drinks at the casino. We had a few drinks and played blackjack, then I left."

The detective asked sarcastically, "Did you win?"

"No, I broke even."

"Good for you, that's a nasty habit. How about Michael, does he gamble a lot?"

Karen was frustrated with the detective by now, "Look, as I said, that was months ago, I don't know what he's doing in his spare time. If you don't mind, I would like to get back to work."

"Detective Roy stood up and walk toward the door and turned around.

"Just one more question?"

"Yes!"

"You wouldn't know anything about the young lady found gagged and tied up in the basement of this building earlier this week, would you?"

The detective pulled out his notepad and flipped the page.

"Judy Wilson! I'm told you were the last person to see her the night she went missing."

"We both worked late that night, but I left before her." The detective placed the notepad back in his jacket pocket and pulled out his business card, and placed it on the desk.

"Well, thank you for your time Karen. If you see Michael, give me a call."

CHAPTER 26

Desmond sat at the table looking through Rodney's files. The guard opened the door and escorted Rodney to the chair.

"Who the hell are you?" Rodney asked as he sat down.

"Mr. Jackson, I'm your attorney, Mr. Taylor, Desmond Taylor."

"My attorney!" Rodney said, looking Desmond up and down.

"Yes! Didn't your girlfriend Trina inform you I was coming?"

"Trina!"

Desmond looked at Rodney with a little suspicion.

Rodney laughed.

"Oh! My lady Trina. Yeah my bad, I have been locked up so long. You know what I mean?"

"No! I don't!"

Rodney gave Desmond a look of disgust.

"So when am I getting outta this hell hole?"

"Calm down, Mr. Jackson! This isn't an easy case. I've been reading your files and some things don't quite add up, but believe me, I'll get to the bottom of it."

"That's good to hear cause I was set up!"

"Is there anything I should know Mr. Jackson? Anything that could hurt this case?"

"Naw man!"

Desmond wasn't sure he fully believed Rodney.

"Are you sure?"

Rodney got a little agitated, "What did I just say?"

"Ok, I need you to know to do my job, we have to establish some trust. So, when the cops arrested you, did they tell you why?"

Rodney smirked, "Man, these crooked ass cops! You'll be

131

lucky if they read you your Miranda rights before choking you half to death are pressing their knee in your neck until you can't breathe."

"There could be a way around that, seeing how the police aren't as credible as they use to be, especially towards black men. And they don't have any physical evidence to tie you to this crime. So give me a few weeks to do some digging, and don't discuss your case with anyone understand?"

Rodney smiled, "Ok boss."

Desmond began to gather his things and put on his jacket.

"I'm not your boss, I'm your attorney. Now I agreed to take your case because I was told you were innocent, Mr. Jackson. I hope I'm not wasting my time."

Rodney said sarcastically, "Everything is on the up and up, Mr. Taylor."

"Good!"

"So you got a lady at home? Desmond hesitated to answer, wondering why he asked such a personal question."

"Yes, we're engaged and we will be having a baby soon."

"Congratulations! She must really be someone special," Rodney smiled.

"Yes she is."

"Well, tell her, I said thank you!"

Desmond looked confused. "Thank you! For what?"

"Well, I'm sure with a baby on the way and planning a wedding, she'll have her hands full. I'm sure that can get lonely."

"We'll manage."

Rodney thought to himself, stupid ass nigga!

"I'm just saying, this case is going to take up a lot of your time."

132

Desmond was agitated by this time, "As I said, we'll manage!"

"My bad! I didn't mean to get you all worked up. I'm just trying to get to know you. Ain't you the one that said we gotta trust each other?"

"Yes, about the case, not my personal business. Guard!"

Karen picked up her phone and dialed out.

"We got problems."

"What's the problem?"

"A detective just left my office. He asked me some questions about you and Judy. He told me if I ran into you to call him. You can't come home right now. You need to lay low."

"I can hang out with my brother, but you will need to drop me off some clothes."

Later that evening, Stephanie sat at her desk. She talked to herself out loud"

"I can't believe my sister, then again I can. She is so fucking judgmental even after all I have been through."
Judy was in the guest room and overheard Stephanie having a conversation. She got up off the bed and walked to stand at Stephanie's door and knocked.

"Come in," Stephanie said as she looked up.
Judy opened the door; she stood there in her robe.

"You still working?"

"Yes, I'm sorry, did I wake you?"

"No, I wasn't asleep but I heard you in here, and I wasn't sure if you were on the phone. You sounded so upset. Is everything okay?"

"Yes, I'm fine. It's just sibling stuff."

"I understand. Well, if you want to talk, I'm here for you. It's the least I can do considering all you have done for me."

Stephanie blew out a deep breath.

"I'm fine. Thank you though. I'll be okay."

"All right, the offer stands if you change your mind."

Visibly upset. Suddenly she interrupted Judy.

"It's just that she made me feel as if I was the reason Desmond asked for a divorce."

"Oh sweetie, I'm so sorry. That must be very upsetting for you."

"Yes it is, but it shouldn't. We have never really gotten along, but she is my sister. I expected her to be somewhat supportive, understanding... a little sympathetic maybe. But I see she is still her old judgmental self."

Judy held Stephanie's hand and looked her in the face.

"I understand. It's hard sometimes when the people you love hurt you. That's part of life, as you now know, especially with the divorce. But sometimes you have to let those people who hurt you, go."

"How can I let my sister go? I mean just because we are not close and..."

Judy sat on the sofa and cuts Stephanie off.

"I know, but sometimes regardless of relation, you got to feed people like that with a long-handled spoon. I'm not saying cut em out of your life, just love them from a distance. How else are you gonna have some peace of mind?"

Stephanie got up from her chair and sat next to Judy on the sofa.

"I hear you. It disappoints and frustrates me when a family does this."

"Yes, and you know all about how to deal with disappointments in your profession. Sometimes you must deal with it in your personal life the same way. Especially when you know people mean you no good."

"You know Judy... you're right. I've gone through a lot

lately, both professionally and personally. From now on, I'm going to do what makes me happy and not care about those who hate on me and don't support me."

"That's what I like to hear. You're a beautiful, strong, and smart woman."
Judy nudged Stephanie with her elbow playfully and smiled.

"Now start acting like it."
Stephanie smiled bashfully and looked into Judy's eyes.

"Thanks for listening and being here for me."
Judy embraced Stephanie.

"You're welcome."

CHAPTER 27

At the kitchen table Desmond and Candice were having dinner. "I can't believe I even agreed to handle his case. He was a pure jackass! You better tell Trina to talk with him, or he will be handling his own damn case.

"What did he say?"

"He was trying to pry into our business instead of worrying about his case and how I was going to get his ass off."

"I will talk with Trina and have her talk with him. In the meantime, can we talk about us?"

"What about us?"

"Desmond, I would like to be married before I start showing. You know how some people can make you feel about this situation. Also, when am I going to meet your parents?"

Desmond got up from the table. "I'll be right back."

Desmond walked back into the room with a black box in his hand behind his back. He walked over to Candice and got down on one knee. He pulled the box from behind his back and opened it.

"Candice, I know things have happened pretty quickly between us. But I am the happiest man alive right now knowing that you are carrying my seed. Will you do me the honor of being my wife?"

Candice screamed. "Oh my God! I thought you would never ask me! Yessss, I will marry you!"

Desmond stood and placed the ring on her finger and kissed her. Candice looked at her ring, "I love it! I love it!"

Stephanie was on the phone as she walked into the house. Judy sat at the kitchen table crying.

Stephanie was so excited. "You should have seen their

faces when Todd hit them with..."
Stephanie sees Judy crying.

"Hey, let me call you back! Judy, what's wrong?" Stephanie asked as she walked over to her.

"It's Mrs. Augustine."

"What happened?"

"She's dead!"

"What! How?"

"She was found suffocated to death."

Stephanie was shocked, "Oh my God! Her poor husband."

"This is all my fault."

"Why would you say that. This isn't your fault."

"It is, if I wasn't over there none of this would have happened.

"Judy you don't know that. This could have happened to anyone."

"Don't you find it strange that I got kidnapped, and the man that saved me wife ends up dead?"

"Look, you don't know that for sure, so let's not jump to conclusions."

"What if the killer was looking for me instead?"

"Judy I need you to stop thinking like that."

"It makes sense, he came looking for me, I wasn't there, he killed her instead. When I was locked in that room, although, I couldn't see him, his voice was very scary. I'm sure that's how Mrs. Augustine felt, scared."

Stephanie walked to the counter, grabbed the liquor, and poured her and Judy a glass.

"Everything is going to be fine ok! Now drink this, it will help you to relax."

Stephanie was in bed and Judy was asleep on the couch. The front door slowly opened. A man walked in dressed in all black, wearing black gloves. He walked over to the couch where Judy was asleep. He grabbed the pillow from the opposite end. He slowly moved the pillow toward

Judy's face. The shadow of the pillow covered Judy's face. As she opened her eyes, the pillow was pushed in her face. She was suffocating. Judy tried to scream, but no sound came out of her mouth. The light came on.

"Hey, hey, it's me! You're ok, you're having a bad dream."

Stephanie grabbed Judy and hugged her. Judy opened her eyes fill with tears.

"He was going to kill me!"

"Shh, no one is going to hurt you."

Todd and Stephanie walked into the courtroom and took their seats. Stephanie didn't know what Todd had up his sleeve, but she hoped whatever it was, it was good.

The judge had been sworn it when Todd stood.

"Your Honor, I would like to cross-examine Mr. John Chris of Charles Schwab."

Mr. Chris walked over and took the stand.

"Mr. Chris, how long have you worked for Charles Schwab?"

"Six years."

"And since you have been there, how many people have you fired because of fraud that you couldn't prove a case against?"

"I object your honor, this is irrelevant to this case."

"Sustained!"

"Does Stephanie Taylor still have any access to these accounts?"

"No, she does not have any access."

"Are you sure?"

"Yes, she is not even allowed to step foot on the premise."

"Okay and if that's true, how was there another transferred made from one of the accounts since Stephanie Taylor does not have access anymore?"

Mr. Chris looked over at his attorney.

"Isn't it true that you made a big mistake by accusing Stephanie Taylor and firing her when the culprit is still employed by Charles Schwab?"

"Uh... Uh..."

"No more questions your honor."

Mr. Chris sat down and whispered something to his attorney.

"Your Honor, may I approach the bench?" Attorney Wright asked.

Attorney Wright had a word with the judge and then walked back to his seat.

The judge looked directly at Stephanie and her attorney.

"After having a brief discussion with Attorney Wright, his client has agreed to drop all charges against your client, Stephanie Taylor. Her job will be reinstated immediately."

Stephanie and Todd looked at each other.

Stephanie whispered, "Aw, hell naw! They are not getting off that easy. I want to file that countersuit."

"I am with you when you're right."

The next day, Stephanie's cell phone rang.

"Good morning, I wasn't expecting to hear from you so soon."

"Good morning. I know, forgive me, but I finished quite earlier than expected with your countersuit documents and thought why not set up a time to go over the details."

"Great, well I'm pretty much free anytime. What does your morning look like? I'm already out and about. I could meet you now if you were available. I'm about 15 minutes from your office."

"Ok, that's perfect. I have to be here for a meeting in a couple of hours so I'll meet you at the coffee shop in the lobby."

"Oh wow, thank you so much!"

139

Later that morning, Stephanie called Judy on her cell phone.

"Judy answered, "Pizza Hut, how may I help you?""

"It's me, Stephanie. I have good news!"

"What is it!"

"I'm going to meet with Todd about my countersuit right now. I can't wait to get some justice."

Judy said sarcastically, "Right, and don't forget to ask him if he'll represent me. I need to file a work hazard lawsuit."

Stephanie walked into the coffee shop just as Todd looked up to see her coming. He stood and pulled out a chair for her.

"Thank you for being such a gentleman."

"You're welcome and I try. Now tell me what you want to drink and eat so I can order us some breakfast. That's if you haven't eaten already?"

"No, I haven't, and thank you."

Todd went and brought back their order.

"Well, thank you again."

Desmond entered the building. He walked into the coffee shop when he heard a familiar voice. When Desmond turned, he saw Todd and Stephanie. He quickly stepped out before being seen. Desmond peeped back in on them before getting onto the elevator.

"I can't believe this shit!" He said as he rode up to his floor. "That mutherfucker!" Desmond paced back and forth in the elevator.

"You come up on my job with my co-worker. Steph, are you serious! Todd, I guess the office gossip got you thinking you can go after my wife. You are about to get served."

A couple of hours later, Todd and a female attorney walked out of their meeting.

"I'm glad that meeting is over, I'm going to the restroom, then I'll meet you for lunch by the elevators." The female attorney told Todd.

"Ok, me too." Todd exited with the other attorneys.
Inside the restroom, Todd stood alone as he washed his hands at the sink.

"Long meeting." He said as Desmond walked in.

"Which one? The one we just got out of, or your previous meeting where you were trying to romance my wife?" Desmond said with anger in his voice.

"As an attorney, the first rule you should know is to get your facts straight. But I'll say this, I'm glad she has a friend like Jason that cares about her... because you are a jerk!"

"Jason, what does he have to do with you trying to put the moves on Stephanie? Is this some sick joke you two are playing?"

"Man, this ain't high school. Nobody's playing games. Wow, you really don't know what's going on with her!"

"She looked fine to me, all smiled up in your face."
Todd shoved Desmond out of his path, Desmond shoved him back.

"This ain't what you want," Desmond said.
Todd moved in close to Desmond.

"It's obvious you don't have who you want?"
Todd's shoulder swiped Desmond as he exited the restroom.

141

CHAPTER 28

Stephanie sat at her desk as she looked over her school assignments when Judy walked in.

"Stephanie, there's someone at the front door."

Stephanie looked at Judy.

"Okay, you know the drill."

Judy headed for the guest bedroom closet as Stephanie went to the front door.

Stephanie opened the door to find Desmond sitting on the porch banister.

"What are you doing!"

"How are you?"

"I'm good."

"Are you really good?"

"Desmond, what are you talking about, and what the hell do you want!"

Desmond moved to stand in front of her.

"I was told that you are going through something, and that's why you were meeting with Todd. So what's going on?"

"Desmond, what I am going through is none of your damn business and if it was, I wouldn't tell you shit!"

"Stephanie, I am still your husband, and believe it or not, I still care about you, and I want the best for you."

Desmond ran his hand down the side of her face. Stephanie stepped back.

"You got fuckin jokes I see."

"Stephanie, please."

"Well, if you must know, my job fired me. They accused me of embezzlement. They believe that since I am going through a divorce, I need money."

"Them motherfuckers!"

"My thoughts exactly!"

142

"Why didn't you come to me to represent you?"
Stephanie looked at Desmond sideways, "Are you serious? After the shit you just put me through, you think I would call you for anything so your white bitch can sit back and laugh at me. Get the fuck outta here. If you cared, you would still be here. You proved to me who you care about, and it ain't me."

Tears began to roll down Stephanie's face.

"Stephanie please, don't cry," Desmond said as he pulled her close to him.

"No, you have to leave," Stephanie said as she moved from his embrace. Stephanie wiped her face and walked inside shutting the door behind her.

The next evening, Todd and Stephanie were sitting in a booth laughing, talking, and having some drinks to celebrate when Jason walked out of the men's restroom. He heard Stephanie's voice, and he turned around to look. He blinked twice to make sure he saw what he thought he saw.

"What!" Jason said to himself. He was surprised to see both of them together.

Jason felt a pang of jealousy run through his body. He continued to watch the two as he stood at the pool table with a few buddies.

"Man, are you going to play, or are you just going to stand there?"

"My bad."

Jason bent down and sized up the balls. He looked over at Stephanie and Todd before taking a shot. The ball bypassed Jason's ball.

"Damn!"

"Well, if you would have paid more attention to what you were doing instead of eyeballing that pretty lady over there, it may have gone in."

"Whatever, I wasn't eyeballing anyone."

After Jason finished his game with his friends, he sat at the bar with his drink when their eyes met. Stephanie smiled and waved him over, but before he had a chance to get up, Marsha walked up and threw her arms around him.
She whispered in his ear.

"You still don't have time for me?"
Stephanie looked over at Jason and Marsha. She couldn't focus on her conversation with Todd. Todd turned to see who she was staring at.

"Ain't that Jason?"

"Yes, I waved him over here, but I guess he's too busy."
Todd laughed.

"I should get going. Todd, thank you for everything." Stephanie said as she stood to leave.
Todd stood and shook her hand.

"I'll be in touch."
Jason looked over just as Stephanie headed for the door.

"Stephanie!" Jason called out. Stephanie stopped, but never looked back. She continued to walk out the door.
Todd looked over at Jason. He laughed and shook his head.

Several days later, Stephanie sat on the couch. She had not heard from Jason since the night at the bar. She picked up the phone and dialed Jason's number.
Jason laid on the bench as he bench pressed some weights while one of his workers spotted him.

"I know you can do more than two hundred and fifty pounds."

"You damn right I can."
Jason's phone rang. He saw it was Stephanie.

"Hey Stephanie."

"Hey, how are you?" Stephanie asked.

"I'm good. How are you?"

"I'm good. I hadn't heard from you. I wanted to call and make sure you were okay."

144

"Oh yeah, I'm good."

You seem distant. Did I do something wrong?" Stephanie asked.

Jason with a serious face. "I was a little disappointed that night at the bar. When you left you didn't even bother to say good night, and you didn't answer when I called out to you. And to be honest, I was surprised to see you and Todd together. Are you guys dating now?"

Stephanie looked confused.

"Are we dating? No, we are not dating. He took me out for drinks to celebrate my win with Charles Schwab. And the reason I didn't say goodbye is because you were busy hugged up with your little girlfriend."

Jason smiled. "No, you have it all wrong. Marsha is not my girlfriend. She hugged me, and that was it. And why didn't you tell me about your win with Charles Schwab?"

"I called you that day to tell you and to see if you wanted to join us for drinks, but you didn't answer, and when I saw you at the bar with her, I figured that's why you didn't answer."

"Steph, come on now. If I was dating her, do you think I would have invited you to the cabin?"

"And why wouldn't you? We're just friends."

Jason laughed. "No comment."

Stephanie walked back and forth with a big smile on her face as she continued to talk with Jason.

"Do you have plans this evening?"

"No, why?" Jason asked.

"I want to do something."

Jason smiled, "Like what?" He only wished she was talking about what he was thinking.

"I would love to go to the movies or even go bowling."

"Naw, you don't want to bowl with me. I'm a champ at bowling."

Stephanie laughed.

"Whatever! Put your money where your mouth is," Stephanie said.

"Bet! What time shall I pick you up?"

"How about six?"

"I'll be there and be ready to pay up."

Candice and Desmond were in the bridal shop. Candice was excited to be shopping for her wedding dress. She smiled nonstop.

"Babe? What do you think about this dress? Babe, babe."

Candice tried to get Desmond's attention, but he stared blankly.

"Desmond! What in the world are you thinking about?"

Desmond was daydreaming about Stephanie. He went back to the scene on the porch when he had visited her the other night. Desmond snapped out of his daze and answered.

"Huh? Did you say something?"

"Yes! I want to know what you think about this dress. I did not like the other one so much."

Desmond was partially attentive to Candice. The scene at Stephanie's front door flashed in his head again.

"Candice, I'm fine with whatever dress you choose. You know I like everything that you wear."

"I know, but this dress is for our special day, and I want to make sure that I look good."

"You will, I just know you will. And why am I here? Isn't it a bad thing for the groom to see the bride in her dress before the wedding?"

Candice looked at Desmond in wonderment. "Oh my God! I never thought about that."

Candice refocused on her dress. She smiled as she turned from side to side. One step closer to getting my boo home, she thought to herself.

"I am just so excited to be your wife that's all I can think about!"

Candice held her hand out and stared at her ring. A picture of Rodney popped into her head, and she remembered him saying, "Don't fall in love with this guy."

Desmond watched Candice as she adored her ring. He saw her in deep thought and realized how beautiful she was, not like Stephanie but in her own way.

"Of course, I want you to feel good. You have our baby inside of you, and you are my soon-to-be wife. I want the best for you, for me, for us."

Desmond realized that Candice was still staring at her ring. He wondered if she even heard what he said.

"Candice... Candice... earth to Candice."

Candice snapped out of her thoughts.

"What? Did you say something Des?"

"I sure did. You mean to tell me that I'm over here pouring my heart out to you, and you did not even hear me? I'm hurt." Desmond playfully feigned hurt and placed both hands on his heart.

Candice put the dress down and walked over to Desmond. She leaned into him where he sat and kissed him. She joined in with his playful act. She spoke in baby talk.

"Oh, I'm sorry. Let's go home and make it better. I know just what to do."

She grabbed his hand and pulled him up. She led the way toward the exit.

Desmond smiled a wide smile and stood up. He followed behind her.

"I know you do Ms. Spencer. I'm ready for you to do it too!"

CHAPTER 29

Outside of Karen's home, the detective sat down the street on the lookout for Michael.

Karen came out of her house with a suitcase and put it in the trunk. She got inside the car and started driving. The unmarked car followed behind her and kept his distance.

Karen never saw the unmarked police car down the street.

Karen pulled up into Michael's brother's driveway.

The unmarked car pulled up two houses down and parked.

"Why did you answer the door? What if it had been the police?" Karen asked Michael.

"How else would you have gotten in?"

"Where's Tony?"

"He and his girl went out for a while."

"Are you good? Do you need anything?"

"Yes, I need this right here," Michael said as he pulled Karen to him, and guided her down the hall as he kissed her. He lifted her blouse up and over her head and unfastened her bra. Just then, they heard a loud bang at the front door.

They both jumped.

"Did anyone follow you here?" Michael asked nervously.

"No, I don't think so."

Karen rushed to put her bra and blouse back on.

"I'll get the door. You stay here and keep quiet."

Karen opened the door to find Detective Roy standing there.

"Can I help you?"

"Is Michael here?"

"What are you talking about?"

"Can I come inside and talk with you?"

"No, I'm busy, and besides, we have already talked."

"Is this where Michael's hiding out at?"

The detective tried to look inside the home.

"No, Michael is not here. I told you before, I don't know where he is at. Why don't you believe me?"

"Can I come in and look around?

"Do you have a search warrant?"

"No, but I can get one."

"Well, then you do that!"

Michael listened to the conversation and panicked. He climbed out the bedroom window and ran around to the side of the house.

He peeked around the house as he saw the detective. He continued to listen to the conversation.

"If I found out you're hiding Michael. I will charge you with aiding and abiding a criminal."

"This conversation is over." Karen slammed the door.

Detective Roy walked down the street to his car and drove off. Michael waited until the detective was out of sight before he hopped into his car and drove off.

Stephanie sat as Judy combed Stephanie's hair in a ponytail.

"Well, I hope you enjoy your bowling date with Jason. I'm glad you have someone to spend time with after all you've been through. And he's sure easy on the eyes too."

"It's not a date. Jason is good company, and he has been cheated on too, so he knows what it feels like."

"No!"

"Yes, even him despite his good looks."

"I'm done."

"Thanks."

Stephanie got a text from Jason.

"Jason is at the light and will be here in a minute. I wish you could join us. I'll tell you about my date when I get back."

"Your date, I thought it wasn't a date."

"Well, you know what I mean."

Stephanie walked out of the room. Judy stood at the bedroom door.

Stephanie yelled to Judy. "I'm leaving, and I'll lock the door on my way out, and if you need me, don't hesitate to call me."

"Ok, good night."

Judy heard the front door close. She turned toward the television. The news caught her attention. There was a sketch of the man the police wanted to question. He had been seen at the home on the day of Joe's wife's murder.

"Why does that sketch look so familiar?" Judy asked herself.

Judy paced back and forth.

"The sketch. No, that sketch is Michael! That is why his voice sounded so familiar. Oh my God! I gotta go, but where? I should've never come here. What if he knows I am here! What if he is out there now!" Judy panicked.

Judy gathered her belongings and wrote Stephanie a goodbye note.

Karen paced back and forth. She pulled out her cell phone and dialed Michael's number.

"I can't believe he followed me. Michael, where did you go?"

"I'm out here in the streets. I had to get out of there and think about my next move."

"Ok, good! Look you have to leave town!"

"I don't have anywhere to go."

"I know, but if he followed me here, he ain't gonna stop until he catches you."

"Ok, give me a few days, and I will be in touch. Love you, bye!"

Karen hanged up the phone as a tear rolled down her face. Michael didn't want to go home to Chicago with his mother, but he may not have a choice.

Detective Roy looked through his notes on his desk as he talked to himself.

"I know he was there. Karen thinks she is smarter than me."

Just then, a detective walked into the office.

"Look, I'm going to need you to cut down on the caffeine."

They both laughed.

"Man, this case is about to drive me to drink."

"Are the any leads?"

"Yeah, one, this Karen! She knows more than she's letting on."

"You want me to put some eyes on her?"

"That might not be such a bad idea. With having the sketch out this evening, I'm sure she's going to make a mistake at some point, and lead us right to him."

"Ok, I'm on it!"

The detective left the office.

Judy put the note on the bed in the guest bedroom. She got her wig out and put it on with her sunglasses. She grabbed her purse and the cell phone and called an Uber.

Thanks to Stephanie she had a prepaid debit card to use for personal needs.

Michael was on his way to the motel. He had planned to lay low for a while when his phone rang.

"Yeah."

"Where my money?" Jojo asked.

"Yo money? I don't owe you, you're just the errand boy!"

"You heard me, don't make me come for you!" Jojo said.

"I just paid a lump sum, muthafucka!"

"Nigga, It doesn't matter you were late and you still late. You better break off some cash, jewelry, or goods because your time is up."

The phone disconnected.

"What! This nigga hanged up on me!"

"Damn! Maybe I can stake Stephanie's place out for a few days for some jewelry. I know she got it. Then I can lay low."

Michael headed over to Stephanie's and sat out front scoping the place out.

Meanwhile, Judy got a message that the Uber driver was out front.

As Michael sat and looked around, an Uber pulled up across the street. He saw a female coming out. As she approached his car, he recognized it was Judy. She opened the back door and hopped in.

When Judy got in, the doors locked. The Uber driver started to drive. As he drove, Judy saw an Uber across the street. She noticed the Uber sign on the dash, and then she looked at her driver's dashboard, and she didn't see a sign. Judy realized she had just gotten into the wrong car.

"Hey, can you stop me at the gas station right on the corner? I need to pick up something real quick?"

The driver continued to drive and said nothing.

Where are you taking me?" Judy asked.

"Somewhere safe."

Judy recognized his voice.

"Michael, is that you? Stop this car right now!" Judy yelled.

Michael continued to drive.

"Why are you doing this?"

"You brought this on yourself. Haven't you heard that

152

old saying, curiosity killed the cat?

Judy eased her phone out of her purse. She saw the missed call from Stephanie.

Stephanie had called Judy from the bowling alley to check on her.

Judy dialed Stephanie's number.

Stephanie's phone rang and went straight to voicemail.

She let the voicemail record their conversation.

"Michael, where are we going, and what are you going to do with me?"

"You will see when we get there."

CHAPTER 30

Hours later, Jason pulled into Stephanie's driveway and parked.

"I'm so exhausted. I don't even think I can move."

Jason laughed.

"See, that's what you get for trying to beat the big dog. You should have stopped after game three."

"You should have stopped me. My arm feels like spaghetti."

"Don't worry, I got you."

Jason got out of the car and walked around to the passenger side, and opened the door.

"I'm sorry, but can you unfasten my seatbelt?"

When they made it to the front door, Stephanie noticed the lights were off.

"I wonder why the lights are off?"

Once inside, Stephanie flipped on the light switch. Stephanie stood and looked around.

Jason grabbed her arm.

"Hey, what's wrong?"

"I don't know. Something doesn't seem right. Let me go check on Judy."

Stephanie walked down the hall with Jason on her heels.

Stephanie knocked at Judy's bedroom door. She knocked a second time, and still no answer. Stephanie opened the door and turned the light on to find the room empty. Stephanie moved further into the room.

"I wonder where she could be?"

"Why don't you call her."

"Right."

Stephanie pulled her phone out and dialed Judy's number. The phone continued to ring. Then she saw the note on the bed and hanged up. She picked up the note and read it.

"She left," Stephanie said as she looked at Jason.

"What do you mean she left?"

"She said she should have never come here. She left because she didn't want to put me in danger.

Stephanie handed Jason the note as she left Judy a voice message.

"Judy, this is Stephanie. Call me as soon as you get this message."

Stephanie turned to Jason.

"Jason, where can she be? I've been so selfish. I should have been here with her."

"No Stephanie, don't you blame yourself. Judy is a grown woman."

"But she wouldn't be in this mess if it wasn't for me."

Stephanie looked at her phone and realized she had a message. Stephanie checked her message and listened.

Stephanie heard Judy talking to Michael.

"Oh my God! Michael, my ex has Judy."

"Are you sure?"

"Yes, I would know that voice anywhere. We have to go to the police."

"But we don't know where they are."

"I can track her with my phone.

At the police station, Stephanie was frantic. She and Jason walked to the counter. The officer saw them and walked up to the glass.

"Can I help you?"

Stephanie was anxious. "My friend has been kidnapped. I believe my ex-boyfriend has her. I don't know what to do."

"Ma'am calm down! The officer said.

Stephanie walked back and forth as she started to cry.

"You need to do something! She's in danger!" Stephanie yelled.

Stephanie gave the officer her phone.

"What is this?" The officer asked.

155

"My phone got dammit! You need to find her. She has a tracker on her phone. Now go and find her! Stephanie said in frustration.

Jason walked up.

"Stephanie, you need to calm down! Officer, her friend called, and we were able to hear what was said. This guy, Michael said he was taking her somewhere, and we think she is in danger. Can you check it out?"

"Wait here!" The officer said.

The officer stuck his head in the door. Detective Roy was on the phone. He waved for the officer to come in.

"Yeah, I'm leaving now, it's been a wild night. Ok bye! Man, whatever it is I'll deal with it tomorrow," Detective Roy said.

Detective Roy walked from behind his desk.

"There's some deranged woman in the lobby, saying her friend has been kidnapped. She said she has a tracker on this phone. She mentioned some guy named Michael took her."

Detective Roy stopped and took the phone from the officer.

"Michael! Where is she?"

"She is in the lobby."

Jason had his arms around Stephanie as she cried with her head laid on his chest.

"If something happens to her, I don't know what I'm going to do."

Detective Roy walked up.

"Hi, I'm Detective Roy. I hear you may have some information about a possible kidnapping?"

"Ain't no possible, my friend has been kidnapped by my ex."

"And who is your ex?"

"His name is Michael Jamison."

"Michael Jamison, are you sure? Why would your ex kidnap your friend?"

"Look," Stephanie said, frustrated, "You are wasting time. I gave you my phone. There is a tracker on Judy's phone. You should be able to find her."
Detective Roy was shocked.

"This wouldn't be the Judy that was found in the basement of Charles Schwab?"

"You know about that?" Stephanie asked.

"Yes, we have a team investigating it."

"Well, she's been staying with me. She wrote me a note saying she didn't want to put me in harm's way. Then she called and left me a voice message. I heard him in the background, and I recognized his voice. He's taking her somewhere."

"And you're positive that it's Michael?"

"Oh, I'm damn sure it is!"

"Do you mind if I keep your phone?"

"That's fine!"

"I'll get it back to you asap! Thank you for this information, and don't worry, I will find her."

"Come on! You need to get some rest."
Detective Roy walked away. He pulled out his phone.

"Hi, I'm sorry! I'm going to be later than expected."

Judy lay with her feet and hands tied to the bed. Her mouth was covered as the tears fell from her face. She continued to move her legs and arms in hopes of loosening the ropes.
Judy heard voices outside the window. She tried to make as much noise as she could with the duct tape over her mouth.
She screamed, "Help me! Help me!"

"Shh! Did you hear that?" The woman outside the motel door said.

"Hear what?"
They stood and listened.
Judy screamed as loud as she could, again.

"It's probably the television."
The man and woman walked past the room.

Jason and Stephanie walked inside. "Man, this has been a night to remember," Jason said.
"And one I want to forget." Stephanie replied."
"I know. Come here. There's something I want to talk with you about."
Stephanie walked over to Jason and took a seat next to him on the couch.
"How comfortable are you staying here by yourself tonight knowing Michael is somewhere out there?"
"I've never thought about it, and besides, I don't think Michael would hurt me."
"You don't know that. Michael has killed and kidnapped someone already. You don't know what state of mind he is in. He may not be the same person that you used to know."
"Yeah, you are right. I never thought he would do any of the things he is accused of doing."
"I don't feel comfortable with you staying here by yourself. At least get a good security system."
"Do you have any suggestion on a good company I can call?"
"I sure do. When are you going to call them?"
"First thing in the morning."
"Okay, in that case, do you mind if I stayed in the spare room tonight?"
"Jason, of course not, we are good friends, so why would I mind? I'll get you some clean sheets and a blanket for you."
Stephanie got up and made her way to her linen closet. She never saw the look of disappointment on Jason's face when she said they were just good friends.

Michael walked inside and sat right down at the bar.

"What's up man, I'll take a beer."

"Alright then. Here you go and that will be $5."

Michael paid the bartender. And as he drank his beer, he heard a loud familiar voice getting closer.

"Yeah, what was that shit you called me on the phone?" Jojo said.

Jojo's friend Tommy walked up and stood near Michael on his right.

"Yeah, I want to hear this," Tommy said.

Jojo walked up on Michael's left, and the guy sitting there got up. Michael stood up, and Jojo pushed him back down on the barstool. He kept his hand on his shoulder.

"Nothing like talking face to face," Jojo said.

Michael pushed his hand off his shoulder and stood up, and got in his face.

"What the fuck you want errand boy? I'm not some punk-ass bitch you gone keep fuckin with. Like I said, I paid mine."

"I don't know what's going on, but you three need to take that shit outside!" The bartender said.

"I'm good. I'm not with him and his errand boy."

Jojo pulled his shirt up a little to reveal his gun to Michael.

"My steal, I, and you are gonna take a walk."

Tommy pushed Michael outside.

"Hurry the fuck up!" Jojo said.

Michael turned around to shove him back, but Tommy raised his shirt to reveal he was packing also.

The men shoved Michael to the back of the building. A truck pulled up, and two other guys jump out. Jojo hit Michael in the face, turned to his partners, and laughed. Michael stumbled back into the other guy As Michael stumbled, he grabbed Tommy from the back. The other guys were right behind Michael hitting him. They pulled him off of Tommy. Michael felt multiple hits all over his body, but he didn't stop defending himself. One of the guy's gun fell and got kicked out of range. He looked for it, and then they heard a gunshot.

"Ahhh, I'm hit!" Jojo said.

Michael held the gun and staggered as he pointed at the men.

Everyone scrambled. The men jumped in the truck and left Michael behind.

Michael stumbled into the shadows. He was too weak to call out for help and passed out on the ground.

CHAPTER 31

Detective Roy looked at Stephanie's phone. He saw the area of the location on Stephanie's phone. Detective Roy went to the break room where a few officers were standing around.

"Hey, I got a lead on the Michael case. I need you guys to follow me."

When the officers made it outside, Detective Roy told Detective Morris to ride with him.

Detective Roy pointed to the other men.

"You guys follow me."

Detective Roy looked at the streets that led up to the location, and then he handed the phone to Detective Morris.

"Here, I need you to let me know if they start to move again."

Michael was on the ground as a couple of men approached him.

"Hey fella, are you okay?"

The second man bent down and moved Michael's face around. Michael came to and looked around.

"Where am..." Michael said as he tried to get up.

"Hey, stay still while I call the paramedics." The second man said.

"No, I'm okay, I'm okay."

Michael got up and was holding his side. He slowly made it to his car in front of the bar. He looked around to see if he saw the men that attacked him.

"Payback's a bitch, you motherfuckers!" Michael yelled.

Michael climbed inside. He opened his glove compartment and grabbed a rag to wipe the blood from his nose and mouth.

Michael looked at his face in the rearview mirror.

I can't believe this shit! Ok, if that's how they want to play.

Michael started the car and headed for the motel. As he approached the motel, he saw the police cars there. He drove slowly past the police.

"Fuck! I got to get the fuck outta here.

Detective Roy stood at the counter. He pulled out the photo of Michael and showed it to the motel manager.

"Have you seen this man?"

The manager looked at the photo.

"Yeah, he checked in earlier with a woman."

"What room?"

The manager looked through the registration book.

"They're in room 102." The clerk said.

"Can you let me in the room, or can you give me the key?"

"And why would I do that? The clerk asked.

The detective showed the clerk his badge. "This man kidnapped the woman with him, that's why!"

"Oh, okay." The clerk handed the detective the key.

Detective Roy left the motel lobby and walked over to tell his men what room they were in.

"Turn off your lights. Let's sneak in on him," Detective Roy said.

The police pulled up to the motel room, cut the ignition. Detective Roy and Morris got out and walked up to the room. The other officers stood back with their weapons drawn.

Detective Roy stood on the right side of the door as Detective Morris stood on the left. Detective Roy inserted the key in the lock. He turned the door slowly, and before he opened the door, Detective Morris counted, and on three, the door opened, and Detective Morris and Detective

162

Roy burst in with guns drawn. They find Judy tied to the bed. Detective Morris ran to the bathroom as Detective Roy attended to Judy.

Twenty minutes later, Detective Roy escorted Judy to his car. Judy was emotional.

"How are you doing?" The detective asked.

"I don't know what to think. This is the second time Michael has kidnapped me, and he hasn't been caught. I'm scared! As long as he is running free, I'm not safe."

"We will catch him, I promise! But we may need to place you in protective custody until we do."

The next morning, Jason stood at the counter in the kitchen as he made coffee when Stephanie walked in.

"Good morning."

Jason turned at the sound of her voice.

"Good morning Sunshine, did you sleep well?"

"No, I didn't. I kept having the same nightmare."

"That's too bad. You should have awakened me. I would have held you while you slept."

Stephanie made a funny face.

"Right!"

"Oh, by the way, I called my friend who works for Stanley Security, and he will be here at noon if that's okay with you?"

"Sure, that's fine."

Jason handed her a cup of coffee.

"Well, I have to get out of here because some of us have to work for a living."

"Yes, well I feel for those people.

They both laughed.

Jason kissed Stephanie on the forehead and headed for the door. Stephanie followed behind him and stood in the door until he pulled off.

Michael was asleep in his car when he heard the sound of a woman's voice.

"Michael, Michael, are you okay?"
She continued to knock on his window.

"What are you doing here? And why are you parked in my driveway?"
Michael opened his eyes to see his mother. He opened the car door.

"Good morning mother."

"Boy! What are you doing here, and how long have you been asleep in your car?"

"Can't a son come and visit his mother. I got here early this morning, and I didn't want to wake you, so I slept in my car."

"Boy, come on in here and get you some breakfast. I'm so glad to see you. How long has it been since you came back home?"

"Mom, I was just here for Christmas."

"Well, it seems like forever to me."
Michael and his mom walked inside the house.

"So how long will you be here?"

"I will be here for a while. I hope you don't mind?"

"No baby. You stay as long as you want," She said as he patted him on the back and handed him a plate of food.

Thomas puts his cup of coffee on Frank's desk. They observed Karen as she walked into Susan's office.

"There go those hens for their morning cackle."
Karen arrived early and went straight to Susan's office. Susan sat behind her desk going over some paperwork when she heard a knock at her door.
Susan looked up.

"Do you have a minute?"

"Sure, come on in."
Karen shut the door and took a seat.

Frank Stared at Susan's closed-door after Karen walked in.

"Helloooo, earth to Frank. What, no comment?" Thomas said as he stared at Frank.

"Oh yeah, I'll have plenty of comments as soon as I get this coffee down."

"You've been zoning out and not yourself lately. Is something troubling you?"

"No, why you say that?"

"You don't even comment to Karen's slick ass mouth like you usually do for one. Even when we make jokes lately, you don't even chime in."

"Just picking my battles that's all, but I assure you I'm fine. Just charging my batteries."

"Haha, well ok if there is anything you want to talk about, you know I'm here like you've been for me."

"Truthfully, the crazy stuff around here."

Karen sat nervously at Susan's desk. "We have a big problem."
Susan shook her head sideways.

"What now!"

"It's Michael. You know that detective I told you about? He followed me to Michael's brother's house yesterday evening. I'm afraid if they catch Michael he's going to sing like a Jaybird about everything."
Susan sat there and stared at Karen with an angry face.

"I knew I shouldn't have gotten involved with you two fuck ups!"

"You could have said no when Michael and I approached you about the situation, but you were gung ho about it when you were getting the money, and now there's a problem you're singing a different tune."
Susan looked up at the ceiling tapping her fingers on her desk. She looked back at Karen.

"I got it! We need to silence Michael before the police

165

get to him."

"What do you mean, silence him!"

Susan rocked in her chair as she looked directly at Karen.

"You know what I'm talking about."

"Susan, how can you ask me to do that? I love Michael?"

"Which one do you love more, Michael or your freedom? You choose."

Frank was interrupted by the sound of Susan's door as it was jerked open, and Karen walked out like a bat out of hell with a scorned look on her face.

"Shut my door!" Susan yelled.

Karen ignored Susan and kept walking.

"What the hell was that about?" Thomas asked

"Need I say more about the craziness around here? Let's talk later," Frank told Thomas.

CHAPTER 32

Stephanie was in the kitchen when she heard the doorbell rang.

She thought it was Jason. "I wonder if he forgot something."

Stephanie opened the door to find Detective Roy.

"Good morning! I hope I'm not disturbing you."

"No, I thought you were someone else. Come on in." Detective Roy walked inside and stood at the door, and looked around.

"You have a very nice home."

"Thank you! So did you find him? Did you find Judy?"

"Yes, we located Judy. She was at a Motel. She was pretty scared, but she is fine."

Stephanie sighed, "Thank God! What about Michael?"

"He wasn't there."

"So this asshole is still running free?"

"Look, we're going to catch him. We know where all his hotspots are now; it's just a matter of time."

Stephanie said in frustration, "But in the meantime, Judy still isn't safe?"

"We have her in protective custody. She's safe."

"I hope you're right!"

"I just wanted to come by and give you the news and to give you this, it was a big help."

The detective handed Stephanie her cell phone.

"I don't see how," Stephanie said.

"Well, at least we have Judy back safe right?"

"Yeah, I guess you're right."

"I'm going to get out of your hair; I have more detective work to do."

"Thank you!"

167

Detective Roy turned to open the door and then turned back around to Stephanie.

"Oh, I forgot to give you this."

Detective Roy handed Stephanie an envelope.

"What's this?"

"Judy asked me to give it to you. Have a nice day."

Stephanie closed the door behind the detective.

Mid-morning, Detective Roy sat at his desk. He leaned back in his chair as he looked at the crime scene board. Detective Morris walked in.

"Hey, I think I got something on this Karen."

"I hope it's more than what I got. Our prime suspect is MIA. I don't want this case going cold. We owe it to this family to put this piece of shit away for good," Detective Roy said.

"I can't rule Karen out for possibly having something to do with Judy's kidnapping. It seems like a big coincidence, don't you think?"

Detective Roy sat up in his chair.

"We interviewed everyone that worked that night, and nothing seemed suspicious. The security guard that worked that night corroborated her story."

"Yeah, but no one checked the security footage.

"We need that security footage," Detective Roy said.

"I'm already on it!"

"Good! Let's get Ms. Karen back in here."

"You think she'll talk?" Detective Morris asked.

"Being charged with accessory to murder has a way of making a person talk."

In the interrogation room that afternoon, Karen sat at the table. She looked around and saw the security camera in the corner ceiling. She wondered who was behind the tinted window.

Detective Roy walked into the room and closed the door.

168

"Sorry to keep you waiting. Can I get you something to drink?"

"No, I'm good! I have already told you I don't know where Michael is."

"Yeah, I know."

"So what am I doing here?"

"I just thought I would give you one more chance to tell the truth."

"Look, I got more important things to do than to play guessing games with you. You're really pissing me off. If I didn't know any better, I would say this is harassment," Karen said in frustration.

Karen grabbed her purse and stood up.

"Ok, let me get right to it! Where were you on the 7th of March at 6 p.m.?"

"I was at work!"

"All night?"

"I left around 7:30 p.m."

"Are you familiar with the entire building at Charles Schwab?"

"I work there, so yes."

"What about the lower level of the building? Have you ever been down there?"

"Yes, I've been down there, no big deal."

"Were you aware your colleague Judy was held hostage in that lower level of that building?"

Karen cleared her throat.

"Um, Judy! No, I didn't know that."

"Is there anything else, detective?"

"No, not at the moment."

Karen quickly grabbed her purse and walked out of the room.

Karen got into her car. She grabbed her phone out of her purse and dialed Susan's number. The phone rang four times before someone picked up.

"Damn, what took you so long to answer. Look, we need to talk!" Karen said with an attitude. "Meet me at the Howl at the moon. I'm heading that way now!"
Karen drove off and turned left at the first exit. She drove for three miles until she came to the Howl at the Moon bar. Karen walked in and looked around. She took a seat at the table in the corner. Minutes later, the waiter walked up.

"What can I get you?" The waiter asked.

"The strongest thing you got."

"You got it!" The waiter said.
Karen looked at her phone to see if she missed any calls. The waiter returned with the drink. Before the waiter could set the drink on the table, Karen grabbed the drink and guzzled it down.

"Bring me another one."
The waiter walked away just as Susan walked up.

"A little early in the day, don't you think?"

"With the stress I'm under, I'm not so sure if that was strong enough."
The waiter returned with the second drink; he set it on the table.

"What can I get you?"

"A glass of water with two lemons."
The waiter nodded his head and walked away.

"You may change your mind after you hear this information."

"Ok, so what was so urgent?"

"The detective questioned me again."

"Ok, so you already told them you and Michael aren't together, so you shouldn't have anything to worry about."
The waiter sat the water in front of Susan.

"Yes, but he didn't ask me about Michael. He asked about Judy's kidnapping."

"Okay, but this doesn't have anything to do with me," Susan said sarcastically.

"Oh, but it does! Are you not aware that her kidnapping ties to the money? So let's not get cocky cause you are just as involved as we are," Karen said with much anger in her voice.

"Where is the proof of that?" Susan asked.

Karen gave Susan an angry stare.

"So this is how you're going to play?"

Susan took a drink of her water, grabbed her purse, and stood up from the table.

"I think our little meeting is over. Enjoy your drink!"

Karen grabbed her drink and guzzled it down with an attitude.

"Ok bitch, this is how you are going to play!" Karen grabbed her phone and called Michael.

"Hello!"

"Michael! Where the hell have you been?"

"Gotcha! Leave me a message, and I'll hit you back."

Karen looked at her phone.

"I don't know where you disappeared to, but you need to call me as soon as you get this message! If y'all think I'm going down by myself, think again! If I go down, we all go down," Karen said as she disconnected the call.

Stephanie sat down, and opened the envelope the detective had given her, and read the letter.

I'm sorry I ruined your evening. Once you left, I saw a sketch on the news of Michael and it filled me with so much anxiety that I just had to get out of your house. I didn't want anyone else to get hurt because of me. Thank you so much for opening up your home to me. Since I'm in the witness protection program, I can't call anyone, so will you please explain to my mom and tell her please don't worry. Her info is at the bottom. I don't know when we will be able to communicate again. Take care.

CHAPTER 33

$\mathbf{S}$**tephanie** decided to pay a visit to Judy's mother. Stephanie pulled into the driveway. She sat for a minute as she looked at her surroundings. When she was ready, she got out of the car and made her way to the front door. Stephanie rang the doorbell.

"Hello. May I help you?"

"Yes. My name is Stephanie Taylor. I worked with your daughter, Judy. May I come in and speak with you about her?"

"Sure, come on in."

Desmond sat as he looked at the paperwork he brought to discuss while he waited for Rodney. He heard the door open and looked up to see Rodney come in as the guards waited outside the door.

"Hey! What's up boss?"

Rodney saw the unpleasant look on Desmond's face. He rephrased his question sarcastically.

"My bad... I mean... How are you, Mr. Jackson? Good to see you, sir."

Desmond looked at Rodney with a straight face. "I'm good, and you?"

"Shit, I'll be good if say you found out I'm innocent."

"Well, I can't tell you that. I just came to let you know that we are still looking into the case."

"So, you have nothing."

"Not exactly."

Rodney asked the question as his patience was waning.

"Well, what EXACTLY do you have Mr. Taylor?"

"That's why I'm here, Rodney."

"What's why you here? Just tell me the truth?"

"I'm here to ask if there is anything you can think of or maybe forgot to tell me about this case."
Rodney spoke with a raised voice.

"Man... what the fuck! I told you everything I know. Those crooked ass cops and this fucked up justice system got me in here!"

"So you're saying that there is no other information you can provide that will help me clear your name."

"Man... naw. I told you everything I know. You the gotdammed hotshot lawyer."
Desmond puts his paperwork in his folder. He was prepared to leave.

"I need you to find whatever the fuck they did to get me in here and used that shit to get me the fuck out of here."
Desmond walked toward the door with a somber look on his face.

"I'm working on it. I will be in touch as soon as I make some progress."
Rodney stared blankly at Desmond as he walked away.

Stephanie sat at her desk going over her homework assignments when her phone rang. She picked up her phone and looked at the caller ID.

"Hey Todd, how's it going?"

"Things couldn't be better. I have some great news for you. Are you sitting?"

"Yes, I'm just going over some homework assignments. Why, what's up?"

"I just got off the phone with Mr. Chris with Charles Schwab. They settled out of court. They are offering you your job back, that's if you want it. They're offering you 300K in the settlement."

"Are you serious?"

"I just sent you an email with all the details. Check it out and let me know if you accept their offer."

"Oh my God! This is the best news I have heard in months."

Stephanie pulled up her emails and opened the one from Todd. She read the email.

"I accept the settlement amount, but they can take that job, and shove it so far up their ass that it will take months to retrieve it!"

Todd cracked up laughing at Stephanie.

"You are too funny."

"Todd, I want to thank you so much for what you have done for me."

"You are more than welcome, Stephanie."

Frank sat at his desk when his co-worker Thomas walked up and stood inside Frank's cubicle.

Thomas whispered, "Have you been in there yet?"

"Been in where?" Frank asked.

"The conference room."

"No, what's going on?" Frank asked.

"They are calling everyone in and asking about some transfers that have been made."

Frank's phone rang. Mr. Chris called Frank from the conference room. He held his finger up to Thomas and answered the phone.

"Hello."

"Frank, can you come to conference room three?" Mr. Chris asked.

"Sure, I'll be right there."

"We will finish this up when I return."

Frank got up from his desk and walked down the hall to the conference room. When he entered, he saw Susan, Karen, Mr. Chris, and two other men. Franks sat directly across from Mr. Chris.

"I guess you're wondering why I called you in here?"

Frank shook his head. "Yeah, pretty much."

"There have been some fraudulent activities going on with some of Stephanie's clients. Do you happen to know anything about that?" Mr. Chris explained.

"No, I don't."

"Will you be willing to take a lie detector test?"

"Sure, no problem."

Mr. Chris slid over a form and a pen to Frank.

"I need for you to sign this form allowing us to administer the test tomorrow at 9 am."

Frank signed the form and left the conference room.

Frank walked back to his desk. He stood up and looked over Thomas's cubicle.

"Meet me on the third floor by the vending machines in 2 minutes."

As Frank walked to the elevator, Karen walked out of the conference room and watched Frank. She then saw Thomas get up and walk to the elevator as well.

Thomas met Frank at the vending machines. They stood there talking.

"What's up?" Thomas asked.

"I can't take that test," Frank said.

"Why not?"

"Because I know who's involved."

Just then, Karen got off the elevator. She saw Thomas and Frank at the vending machines.

"Who?" Thomas asked.

Frank was just about to talk when he looked up to see Karen.

"Shhh," Frank said.

Thomas looked up.

"Yes, honey dinner was fantastic. He prepared grilled salmon with mashed potatoes, and fried kale," Frank said.

"What are you two up to?"

"What does it look like?" Frank rolled his eyes.

"He treats me so good."

175

Karen got a can of pop from the vending machines and got back on the elevator.

"Nig-ga who?" Thomas asked.

"That bitch right there. She and Susan framed Stephanie, and they used Judy's computer to transfer the money."

"And how do you know that?"

"I overheard them talking about it in Susan's office last week, and there's more, but I'm not at liberty to say right now."

A couple of hours later, Detective Roy walked back to his desk. He grabbed his coat as he looked over at Detective Morris.

"Let's go. I got the search warrant for Michael."
The detectives pulled into the driveway. As they got out, they looked around at the neighborhood.

"Do you think any of the neighbors would talk to us?"

"I don't know. Let's see how this goes first. We may not need to talk to them."
Gene was sitting in the living room watching TV when he heard a knock at his door. He figured it was Michael.
Gene opened the door and was surprised to see two white men at his door.

"Can I help you?" Gene asked.

"Yes. I'm Detective Roy, and this is Detective Morris. We are here to see Michael."

"I'm sorry, but Michael is not here."

"I have a search warrant to search the premises." Detective Morris said and showed Gene the warrant.

"What is this about?"

"Who are you to Michael?" Detective Roy asked as they walked inside the home."

"Michael is my younger brother. What kind of trouble is he in now?"

"I guess you haven't heard the news. Your brother is wanted for murder and Kidnapping."

Gene dropped into the nearest chair and shook his head.

"Are you serious? Who did he murder and kidnap?"

"He murdered Mrs. Augustine and kidnapped Judy Jones." Detective Morris said.

"I followed Karen here yesterday, but she wouldn't let me in so I got a search warrant."

"Well, you are welcome to search my home because he's not here."

"Can you think of any place he would be?" Detective Morris asked.

"If he's not with Karen, no," Gene said.

"So, they're still together?"

"Yes."

"I knew she was lying." Detective Roy said.

After the detective left, Gene phoned his mom.

"Hey Mom, how are you doing?"

"I'm doing good sweetheart. How are you?"

"Mom, are you sitting down?"

"No, Gene why?"

"Some detectives just left my house. They had a search warrant. They said Michael murdered and kidnapped someone."

"Oh no. They must be mistaken. Michael is here, and you know he wouldn't do that, Gene. You did tell them that, right"

"Mom, you know how Michael is. I wouldn't put anything past him."

"Gene, Michael is your brother, and family stick together at times like this."

Gene shook his head.

"Mom, your baby boy is wanted for MURDER, did you not hear me? This is not some petty theft case. He took someone's life!"

"But Gene, we don't know if he really did this. You know how the police are always trying to frame black people for something."

"Okay Mom, but tell Michael not to come back to my place."

CHAPTER 34

Jason was in his office at the gym going over paperwork when Marsha appeared at the door.

"Hello, I need a personal trainer."

Jason looked up to find Marsha standing there. He smiled.

"Well, you can fill out a form so that I'll know if you have had any injuries," Jason said.

"The only injury I have is my heart has been broken, so my trainer needs to be sensitive and understanding to my needs."

"Okay well, Shelby would be great to assist you."

Marsha cut him off.

"Come on Jason, you know I want you to train me."

"I happen to know you have a solid workout routine and don't need a trainer."

"Do you have any pointers?" She said as she looked at Jason's crouch.

"Pointers?"

"Yes pointers, I don't want to get bored, and I need to mix it up."

Marsha started to stretch in front of Jason. She moved over to him and put her leg over his. She proceeded to do squats on his lap.

"Haha, you never cease to amaze me."

Desmond sat on the sofa with Candice as she laid up against him. Desmond looked at the top of Candace's head.

"So what did you do while I was away today?"

Candice looked up into Desmond's eyes. She smiled.

"Thank you for asking. I finished up the last-minute details for my dress alterations. I was able to order the floral arrangements as well. Other than that, not much."

"Well that is enough. That sounds stressful to me, figuring out the details of this flower versus this color, that color. Too much information and too many details."

"Des, it is the same thing you do at work, just different details and different information. Besides, it is very exciting for me! I'm about to be your wife."
Desmond rubbed the top of her head.

"Yeah, I guess you're right. My brain doesn't work with details about flowers and all that stuff."

"I know babe, that's why you left it up to me. I got this, and you got the lawyer stuff!"

"How did it go with Rodney today? Was he calm today?"

"He tried to be calm, but he still had this vibe about him that I don't like. My gut tells me to leave him the fuck alone, and let him find someone else to handle his case."

"Desmond, you can't. That would break Trina's heart."

"Do I look like I give a rat's ass? Hell, I don't even know her."
The doorbell rang.

"Oh, that must be the pizza delivery guy."
Minutes later, Candice and Desmond sat at the table eating dinner.

"Damn! These wings are good."

"I know."
The doorbell rang again. Candice got up, but Desmond stopped her.

"No, you sit. I'll get it."
Desmond walked to the front door and opened it to find the UPS guy.

"I have a package for Desmond Taylor."
He handed Desmond the package.

"I need your signature here."
Desmond signed and handed the clipboard back to the UPS

180

man. "Have a nice evening," Desmond said as he shut the door. Desmond walked back to the kitchen where Candice sat waiting for his return.

Desmond sat at the table as he opened the package. Candice's eyes were glued to the package.

Desmond pulled out the paper and realized it was the divorce decree. Candice saw the change in his face.

"What's wrong Desmond?"

Candice moved to stand next to Desmond.

"So, it's final. I thought that's what you wanted."

Candice walked back to her seat.

"Don't get me wrong, it's just I never pictured myself with anyone other than Stephanie. I'll be right back."

Desmond wanted to check on Stephanie. He wanted to make sure she was okay. Desmond walked back to their bedroom and shut the door. He pulled out his phone.

Stephanie was sitting in her office when her phone rang.

"Hello Stephanie."

"Hey Desmond."

"So, you got what you wanted," Desmond said.

"No, you got what you wanted," Stephanie replied.

Stephanie wiped her eyes with her hand. Desmond paced back and forth with his hand in his pocket.

"Are you okay?"

"Why do you care, Desmond! I gotta go!"

"Steph…"

Stephanie disconnected the call.

That evening, Candice's phone rang as she lay next to Desmond as they watched television. She picked it up hoping it wasn't Rodney calling.

Candice listened to the operator as she asked if she would accept the call from an inmate at the correctional facility. She got off the couch and walked into the bathroom.

"I accept." She said as she ran the water in the sink.

"Hey... Rodney! It's so good to hear your voice."

"Rodney! Since when you start calling me that?"

"Baby, you know I was just playing. I miss you so much."

"Yeah, you better miss me. I can't stand being locked up in here. Not to mention this nigga Desmond all up in you, and I can't do nothing bout it."

"Speaking of Desmond, I need you to focus on the big picture. You gon fuck it up for all of us you keep acting an ass," Candice said.

"Hey, I was trying to feel him out and to see how into you he is. I don't like this shit as it is. I want to make sure you ain't into that nigga like he is into you."

"Baby, you know I love you. Can't nobody replace you, but if you don't chill, your ass gon be in there."

"What that mean? What you talking bout?"

"I mean, you are doing way too much. He told me on his first visit you asked if he had a woman. And that he was going to be spending so much time away from me. Why would you tell him to tell me to thank you? Then this last visit, you had some kind of attitude. He's not feeling you as it is so stop the bullshit!"

Rodney laughed.

"Now THAT, was me being me. I meant that shit too baby. What I wanna know is when am I getting out?"

"As I said, you keep up all this nonsense, and you gonna be in there. I haven't heard anything yet, but I know he is working long hours, though. I don't wanna ask him about you anymore. He is suspicious enough already. I'll let him reach out to you."

"Okay, but he bet not take too long. I hate being in this fuckin place. I can't wait till I can be with you and get all up in that like he is. This shit be fucking with my head man."

"Babe, it's okay, you can't let it get to you. I ain't going nowhere, I swear. You have to think about what's at stake. I love you!"

"I love you too baby!"

Candice walked out of the bathroom and rejoined Desmond.

"Were you on the phone in there?" Desmond asked.

Candice looked like a deer caught in headlights.

"Yes, it was the lady from the bridal shop."

"Is everything okay?"

"Yes, everything is coming along as planned. Thanks for asking. You're so sweet and considerate."

Desmond was trying to get Stephanie off his mind, so he had to talk about something.

"Oh, by the way, my parents invited us over for dinner tomorrow evening."

"And you're just now telling me."

"I'm sorry babe, I forgot."

CHAPTER 35

Stephanie lay in the tub covered in bubbles. She moved her hand back and forth across the bubbles. She lifted her hand to her face, which was covered in bubbles, and blew. Her phone beeped, and there was a message on the screen from Jason. She looked over at the phone, then continued to blow bubbles from her hand.

When Stephanie was finished, she walked into her bedroom and tossed her phone on the bed. She unwrapped the towel from her body and threw it on the bed. She grabbed her robe and put it on as her phone rang again.

"Hello."

"Stephanie! Hey, how are you doing?"

"I'm ok Jason, what's up?"

Jason felt something different with Stephanie.

"Are you ok? You don't sound well."

"I'm fine."

Jason didn't press the issue.

"Did you get my text?"

"I'm sorry, I was in the tub and drifted off to sleep."

"Oh, I understand. A nice warm bath can do that to you. I'm glad you were able to relax. I was wondering if my boy came by and installed that security system?"

"Yes, he did. I can't thank you enough for all your support Jason."

"You know it isn't any trouble at all. Well, I was hoping to come by tonight, I can pick up some Chinese?"

"Jason, I'm not in the mood right now, maybe some other time."

"Sure, I understand. Are you sure everything is ok?"

"Yes, I'm sure. Thank you for checking on me, you're a good friend Jason. I'll call you another time. Goodbye."

Jason looked at his phone confused.

An hour later, Jason was sitting on the couch with a beer in one hand and his phone in the other hand when he heard a knock at the door.
Jason got up off the couch and walked to the door. He opened the door to find Marsha standing there.

"Hey, what are you doing here?" Jason asked.

"I hope you're hungry because I brought dinner."
Marsha held up the bag with food.

"Well since you brought food, come on in."
Jason and Marsha sat around the island as they ate.

"This is exactly what I had a taste for, Chinese food. How did you know I wanted this?"
Marsha smiled. She couldn't tell him about the recording device she placed in his living room behind the television the last time she was there. She was able to hear all of his conversations.

"See, I know exactly what you need and when you need it."

"Jason shook his head. Do you ever give up?"

"Nope. Not when it's something I want."
Jason and Marsha moved to the living room and sat on the couch as they watch television. Jason had another beer while Marsha sipped on a glass of wine.

"Jason, what's wrong? You don't seem like your chipper self this evening?"

"Um... I've got some things on my mind."

"Well you know these hands here can make you forget all about your problems."
Marsha held her hands out and Jason laughed.
Marsha set her wine down and removed Jason's beer from his hand. She straddled him on the couch and began to run her fingers through his hair massaging his scalp.

"Damn! That feels good."
Marsha made her way down to his shoulders. She began to rub his shoulders.

Marsha said seductively, "You're hard as a rock. Why don't you take off your shirt so I can let these hands work their magic?"

Jason eyed her suspiciously. Marsha sat down on his lap and continued to massage his shoulders. Jason laid his head back on the couch and closed his eyes.

Marsha slowly moved her hand down to one of his nipples and rubbed it until it became hard. Then she moved over to the other one. She whispered into his ear.

"Is this helping you to relax?"

"Yes!"

Marsha moved her mouth down to his nipple and replaced her hand with her mouth.

"How does this make you feel?"

Jason moaned, "Good." He grabbed hold of her hips and began to grind into her.

Marsha felt the bulge in his pants and reached her hand down. She removed his penis from his sweatpants. She ran her hand up and down as the pre-cum sipped out.

"Take your pants off. I want to make you more relaxed."

Marsha got on her knees, grabbed hold of his penis, and made him disappear into his mouth. Jason lay there as the feeling took control. He licked his lips, and then his phone rang. Jason grabbed the phone when he saw it was Stephanie without thinking.

"Hey. Um... shit!"

"What are doing? Are you okay?"

Jason moans again, "Aw shit! Marsha!"

Stephanie looked at the phone.

"Jason, I will talk with you later!"

"Steph no!"

Stephanie disconnected the call. She lay across her bed wondering what the hell was going on. Was Marsha over, and were they fucking?

Marsha got up off her knees and smiled.

186

"Are you relaxed now? I know Stephanie can't make you feel like that!"

Jason got himself together. He went to the bathroom with his phone and dialed Stephanie back.

Jason stood as the phone rang three times.

Stephanie still lay across her bed when her phone rang. She looked at her phone and saw it was Jason. She let it go to voicemail.

On the fifth ring, Stephanie's voicemail came on.

"Stephanie, I want to apologize for what you heard. When you have time, please give me a call back."

Stephanie lay across her bed.

"Now, I know I am not crazy. I heard him call out Marsha's name."

Stephanie got up, dressed, and headed out the door.

Twenty minutes later, she pulled up and saw Jason's car. She pulled into Jason's driveway.

Jason and Marsha sat on the couch as they watched a movie when the doorbell rang.

Marsha looked over at Jason. "Are you expecting company?"

"No. I wasn't even expecting you."

Jason got up and headed for the door.

Jason opened his door to find Stephanie on his doorstep. Stephanie pushed her way inside and saw Marsha.

"Oh, I'm sorry. I didn't know you had company."

Stephanie looked up at Jason and turned and walked out.

"Stephanie wait!" Jason yelled as he followed behind her. "It's not what you think."

"Jason, you don't owe me an explanation. You are grown and single. You can do as you please," Stephanie said as she looked back at Jason.

"Maybe I don't want to be single anymore."

"Well, I'm sure Marsha will be glad to know that."

187

The next evening, Desmond and Candice arrived at his parents. "Mom and Dad, I would like for you to meet my future wife, Candice Spencer."
Desmond's father embraced Candice and kissed her on the cheek.

"Welcome to the family," Desmond's father said.

"Nice to meet you," Mrs. Taylor said as she looked Candice up and down.
As they sat around the dinner table eating, Mrs. Taylor was dying to ask Candice a million and one questions.

"Well Candice since I hardly know anything about you. Where are you from? Tell us a little about your family?
Candice was hesitant to answer.

"I was born and raised here on the Southside. My parents and I aren't close, and I have no siblings.

"What about employment? What is it that you do?"

"I'm unemployed at the moment. Living off my severance and my savings."

"Mom! That's enough. We are here to eat, not play 20 questions," Desmond said.

"Okay babe, but am I allowed to ask about my grandbaby's due date?"

"My due date is December 20th."

"Boy or girl? Or do you know yet?"

"No, I don't know yet, but I plan to have a baby reveal party."

An hour later, Desmond and Candice stood at the door to leave.

"Thank you so much for the dinner invite. The food was fabulous," Candice said.

"Thank you! And you are welcomed here anytime."
The ride home was quiet until Candice spoke, "I don't think your mom likes me too much."

"That's my mom. She doesn't think anyone is good

enough for her only son. She didn't like Steph either, so don't let that bother you."

"So, it's okay that she doesn't like me because she doesn't like Steph either. Why does Stephanie always have to be in our conversation? Damn! Desmond, are you still in love with her?"

"I'm not even going to go there with you," Desmond said. "No, I am going to go there with you. We were married for ten years and together for 12. Do you think my feelings are just going to change like that for her? Huh, Candice? It's obvious you have never been in love with anyone."

Candice sat there quietly. She couldn't say what she really wanted to say. "You're right, I'm sorry," Candice said.

Back at the Taylors, Mrs. Taylor stood at the kitchen sink doing the dishes while her husband put the food away.

"Nothing but trash!" Mrs. Taylor said.

"Honey, you hardly even know her," Mr. Taylor said.

"Oh, I forgot, just because she's white she's right. What was I thinking? " She said sarcastically.

Mr. Taylor shook his head.

"Father like son, I see. I remember years ago, when you did me the same way Desmond did Stephanie, but the only difference was I had kids so I stayed."

"You will never let me live that down, will you?"

"Nope, because that's something I never want you to forget. I never want you to forget how much pain that caused me."

Sunday night, Frank couldn't sleep. He couldn't stop thinking about the information he had and what he needed to do with it. He tossed and turned until sleep fell upon him, and when he awoke the next morning, he knew what he needed to do.

189

Monday morning, Desmond picked up his phone and dialed the private investigator's phone number.

"Hello, Slay Investigation Services, How Can I help you?"

"Hello Mrs. Jones, how are you? This is Desmond Taylor.'

"Mr. Taylor, hello! I'm fine. How are you?"

"I'm doing well. Thank you. Is your husband around?"

"Yes, he's in his office. I will connect you."

"Hello, this is Marcus."

"Hey! Marcus, Des."

"So what's good? How's life after divorce man?"

"I'm actually engaged to be married, and I do have a child on the way."

"Wow! Really? Congrats, Des. I really mean that. I hope that you are really happy. I know you always wanted kids."

"Yeah, Candice and I are really happy."

"Candice huh?" Mr. Slay let it go. He could tell by Desmond's voice that he was lying.

"Yeah, Candice Spencer. Soon to be Mrs. Taylor."

"Well, if you're happy, I'm happy."

"Yeah man... but I wanted to ask you for a favor. I need help with the pro bono case I'm working on."

"For sure man. What do you need?"

"I'm working on this case, and I have no additional information to help prove this client is innocent."

"You need me to do some digging?"

"This is going to take more than just digging. This case is going to need some footwork."

"Okay, so just send me the information, including where you want me to go, and I'll be on it as soon as I assign these other cases I have."

"I just need you to track down some names and do some footwork to find some of his and former crew members.

190

Hopefully, they'll provide some info on another murder of a particular drug dealer. I'll send all that over to you right now."

"Alright man... you take care now, I'll be in touch with you soon."

"Thanks... I look forward to it. Bye."

That morning at work, Frank sat at his desk. He pulled out his phone and sent a text message to Thomas.

"Hey, what's up?" Thomas asked as he walked into Frank's cubicle.

"I have to do it. I have to tell HR what I know."

"Do you think that's wise?"

"If it were you, wouldn't you want someone to come forward and clear your name?"

"Yes, but why does it have to be you?" Thomas asked.

"Who else would it be?"

"How do you know you can trust Mr. Chris's old white ass?"

"I don't."

"Well, just be careful."

Frank exited the elevator and nervously looked around to see if anyone was in the hallway as he followed the sign towards HR.

Frank walked up to the receptionist.

"Hi, I don't have an appointment, but I need to speak with Mr. Chris it's urgent. My name is Franklin Bonds."

"Mr. Chris doesn't usually see people without an appointment, but let me check with him. You can have a seat, and I'll let him know you're out here."

"Ok, thank you."

Frank sat down and waited in the lobby.

The receptionist walked back out to the lobby where Frank was sitting.

"Mr. Bonds, you can go on in."

Mr. Chris stood and extended his hand out to shake Frank's hand with a smile.

"Hello Mr. Bonds. How may I help you?"

"I have some information that will hope with the fraud investigation."

"Oh really. Well in that case have a seat."

"Mr. Chris, you asked me yesterday about taking the lie detector test and I signed the form to take it, but now I can't take it."

"And why is that?"

Frank rocked back and forth in his chair. He was nervous. He didn't know if he could trust this man or not.

Karen and Susan stepped off the elevator and looked around the hall as they headed for Mr. Chris's office.

"I know he's in there. I overheard him and Thomas talking this morning."

"What's the problem Frank? You can trust me."

Mr. Chris leaned forward and looked Frank in the eyes.

"Are you involved?"

"No, but I know who is."

Just then, they heard a knock at the door. Frank looked at the door and back at Mr. Chris.

"Sir, no one can know I am here!" Frank said nervously.

"You'll be okay."

Mr. Chris got up and walked over to the door and opened it.

"Well, well, what brings you ladies, here? Come on in ladies. Frank here was just about to tell me who's involved in the embezzlement."

When Mr. Chris turned around, the conference room door was cracked open and Frank was gone.

192

End of Part 1

BETRAYAL

www.ingramcontent.com/pod-product-compliance
Lightning Source LLC
Chambersburg PA
CBHW070515260626
47161CB00004B/1554